# CONTENTS UNDER
# PRESSURE

# CONTENTS UNDER PRESSURE

Lara M. Zeises

**Delacorte Press**

Published by
Delacorte Press
an imprint of
Random House Children's Books
a division of Random House, Inc.
New York

Visit us on the Web! www.randomhouse.com/teens
Educators and librarians, for a variety of teaching tools, visit us at
www.randomhouse.com/teachers

Library of Congress Cataloging-in-Publication Data

Zeises, Lara M.
Contents under pressure / Lara M. Zeises.
p. cm.
Summary: Lucy, a fourteen-year-old high school freshman, experiences the
happiness and confusion of dating a popular older boy, changing relationships
with life-long friends, and sharing a bedroom with her older brother's
pregnant girlfriend.
ISBN 0-385-73047-0 (trade)—ISBN 0-385-90162-3 (GLB)
[1. Interpersonal relations—Fiction.   2. Family problems—Fiction.
3. Brothers and sisters—Fiction.   4. Pregnancy—Fiction.   5. High
schools—Fiction.   6. Schools—Fiction.   7. Delaware—Fiction.]   I. Title.

PZ7.Z3938Co 2004
[Fic]—dc21
2003005411

Printed in the United States of America

April 2004

10 9 8 7 6 5 4 3 2 1

BVG

*For Laurie, who's been there since page one,
and for Lisa, without whom there
would be no page one*

# CONTENTS UNDER
# PRESSURE

# Chapter 1

Friday, 8:33 P.M. My best friend, Allison, and I have set up camp on the industrial-carpeted floor of her mostly refinished basement and, at the moment, are in the process of giving ourselves disco-orange pedicures. We picked orange because Halloween is only a couple of weeks away, and since we both feel that we've outgrown the whole trick-or-treating thing, it's our way of honoring our formerly favorite holiday.

Allison caps the bottle and passes it to me. "Hey, Lucy," she says. "I kind of have to tell you something, but I don't want you to get mad at me." I can't think of a single bit of welcome information that's ever followed an introduction like that, so I hold my breath while she blows on her sloppily painted toenails.

"So what is it?" I prompt her.

Ally looks up at me through a fringe of strawberry-blond bangs, a semiworried look plastered on her pale, heart-shaped face. "I think I have a crush on Brad Thomas."

I wait for her to finish her statement but nothing follows. "Yeah, and?"

"That's it." She twirls a piece of her stick-straight

1

hair around an unpainted pointer finger, the nail of which has been chewed to the quick. "I have a crush on Brad Thomas." Ally says each word slowly, emphasizing every other syllable.

"Oh. Well, good. Good for you."

I shake the bottle of polish, making sure the flecks of glitter are distributed evenly, and then carefully begin to apply a second coat to my toenails. Allison's face scrunches slightly, like she's disappointed I didn't have more of a reaction.

"So it's okay?" she says. "You're not mad?"

"Why would I be mad?"

Allison gives me her confused look, the one where her bottom lip pushes to the left and her right eyebrow arches slightly. "Well," she says, in a slightly tentative voice. "I know you sort of had a thing for him last year."

"What!" I practically yelp, smacking her knee. "*He* had a thing for *me*, remember?"

"Whatever," she says. "So it's cool then? Me liking him?"

"I'm not mad about it," I say, grinning. "But I don't know if liking Brad Thomas could ever be considered *cool*."

Allison picks up a nearby throw pillow and beams it at my head, but she knows I'm only teasing. We've been best friends since kindergarten, when I showed up on the first day without a snack and she generously donated half of her apple and an iced oatmeal cookie. In the nearly ten years since, there have been only a few dozen times where one of us hasn't spent Friday night at the other's house. Our current rituals consist of painting our nails, giving ourselves facials with thick, foul-smelling green mud we squeeze from a tube, watching videos (our favorite, like *Grease*), and eating cookie dough right out of the package.

Allison removes the ribbon of toilet paper she's wound between her toes. "So what do you think the Kims are doing tonight?" she asks.

I shrug. "Who cares?"

"I do," Ally says. "I mean, don't you think it's weird that we never hang out with them anymore? And how about Tabitha? Have you seen her hair? She looks like she was made over by the freak fairy."

There used to be five of us who did everything together, but between our eighth-grade graduation ceremony and freshman orientation this September, just about every friend I had went through some sort of transformation. First Kim Talbot joined the cheerleading squad, trading several IQ points for a pair of black-and-silver pom-poms ("Cute boys don't date girls who seem smarter than they are," she informed me). Then Kim Tate, who used to do everything Kim #1 did, bucked that trend by making goalie on the second-string field hockey team. Tabitha, our floater friend (i.e., good friends with all four of us but not really best friends with any of us—or anyone else for that matter), spent the summer in Manhattan with her older sister, Elizabeth, and came back some kind of alterna-chick. Translation: she dyed her hair fuchsia, bought a pair of tough-girl motorcycle boots, and started listening to the kind of loud techno music that gives me headaches.

Then there's Allison, who hasn't really changed all that much but who's totally shaken by the "breakup" of our group. I guess I'm a little upset about it, too—we've all been friends since forever—but in a way, I feel free. When you have a semipermanent social circle, it pretty much becomes your identity. Like you're one-fifth of a whole, and not five individual people who simply hang out together. And you can't just do stuff without inviting the others because someone always feels left out, which usually leads to a fight and a lot of carefully folded notes passed in study hall.

"I haven't talked to Tabitha in ages," I say. "Not since your party. Did I tell you she's stopped riding the bus?"

Allison shakes her head. "She probably thinks she's too cool or something."

"Maybe."

We're quiet for a minute, and I bet we're thinking

exactly the same thing. How this time last year there would have been three other sets of toenails being painted right now, and how, even if Allison had invited the Kims and Tabitha to hang out with us tonight, they would've said no.

I guess I can't really blame all these changes on after-school activities or Jell-O–colored hair dye. Because what's really come between us is boys.

Kim Talbot, who is what my mom would call an early bloomer, started "dating" in the sixth grade, and Kim Tate followed suit three months later. At the time, it wasn't all that big a deal, because back then going out with someone had very little to do with actually going anywhere. Basically, all you did was hold hands in the hallway and write each other stupid notes with lots of exclamation points every single day.

Then, if you were lucky, there was a dance during the two and a half weeks you were actually boyfriend and girlfriend and the two of you got to do that stupid swaying twirling thing that people who are going out do at dances. Eventually one of you got a crush on someone else, so you broke up, and the girl cried for twenty minutes, even if she was the one who wanted to break up in the first place, and then everyone traded boyfriends and it started all over again.

But now it's . . . different. Kim Talbot started going out with the kicker on the varsity football team last summer, during preseason. He got his license this September and now they go on real dates, like to the movies and restaurants that don't have drive-throughs attached. The other Kim has been practically glued to this tri-season jock Trip Weathers ever since the two of them bumped into each other at the Christiana Skating Rink last July. And Tabitha met an older guy when she was in New York, some seventeen-year-old would-be poet who makes coffee at Barnes & Noble and who promised to send actual letters—not just e-mails—every three *days*.

I never used to care about whether or not boys liked me, but now I feel like some kind of reject. The last time the five of us were really together—in August, at Ally's traditional end-of-the-summer slumber party— we played Truth or Dare and Tabitha asked Kim Talbot how far she'd gone with J.T., the kicker, and Kim said she let him feel her up *four times*. Then Kim Tate asked Tabitha the same question and she said that right before she left New York, Elliot, the coffee-brewing poet boy, put his hand up her skirt and it was nice (nice!) and she would've let him do more but then her sister and her sister's boyfriend came home and messed everything up.

Allison had this look of horror on her face, like "What's happening here?" But *I* was the one the rest of them looked at with pity, because even Allison got kissed by some goober at her cousin's wedding last May.

Yes, it's true. My name is Lucy, but it might as well be Loser since I'm fourteen years old and I've never, ever been kissed.

Not even a peck.

It's not that I don't like boys, or that I'm opposed to kissing them, but boys my age are just so immature. When Brad Thomas had that huge crush on me last year, I thought I might try to like him because at least then I'd have someone to kiss. But then I thought about what it would be like if he was my "boyfriend," and what my big brother, Jack, would think if I ever brought him home. I just knew he'd say, "C'mon, Biscuit. You can do better than that Oxy-moronic dweeb."

I knew he'd be right, too.

"You're so lucky," Allison says later, after our pedicures and facials are complete. "You never even think about boys."

I frown. "I do too."

"Well, you never talk about them."

"Sure I do. Just not all the time. Not like *some* people."

Ally blushes slightly. "So seriously, Lucy—what do you think the Kims are doing tonight?"

"Getting felt up by their boyfriends."

"Lucy!" Allison shrieks.

"I was only kidding."

"I know," she says. "The sad thing is, you're probably right."

"Why is that sad?"

Ally shrugs, lowering her head. "I don't know. It's just . . . different. I'm not, like, *jealous* or anything. But I'm starting to feel . . . I don't know. You know?"

"Yeah," I say. "I think I do."

"C'mon," she says after a brief moment of silence, jumping up and shaking off the seriousness of our previous conversation. "Let's go make some popcorn and watch *Grease*."

I sigh and follow her up the basement steps. Maybe change isn't the problem. Maybe it's the *not* changing that feels so itchy. Jack always used to say that the worst thing to be was stuck. Is that what Ally and I are? Still stuck in the eighth grade?

As the foil on the Jiffy Pop begins to swell with bursting kernels, I make a mental note to talk to Jack about how one goes about getting unstuck. Then I put on my game face and try to look enthusiastic about watching *Grease* for the zillionth time.

# Chapter 2

The next day, Allison's mom takes us to the mall to look for homecoming dresses, which seems sort of futile to me because neither of us has a date and the dance is next Saturday. Right before school started, Ally tried to get me to agree that we'd go regardless, but I'm not that big on dances to begin with—I'm a total klutz—so I kept changing the subject and eventually she dropped it altogether.

It's a little past two, and the mall is jam-packed with overly made-up sixth-grade girls in low-rise jeans and crop tops that show off their faux belly rings. I'm not sure when little kids got so trendy, but I feel completely self-conscious in my worn jeans and Jack's old Haley High sweatshirt.

We duck into one of those overpriced boutiques I never shop in, and Allison starts digging through a rack of frothy pink gowns with no straps. Mrs. Ziegler holds one up to me and says, "Lucy, this is *definitely* your color. Why don't you try it on?" I don't have the heart to tell her that it doesn't matter how "me" the color is, there's no way my practically nonexistent chest is going to come close to filling that thing, so I just take the dress from her and shuffle off to fitting room number three.

A brief word about my breasts: I don't have any. Now, I try not to be the kind of shallow, immature person who obsesses about cup size, but the truth is, there's just nothing there.

There was a time, years ago, when I actually hoped I'd never grow boobs. This happened right around the time Jack got his driver's license and his first real girlfriend: Echo Erhard. She was *all* boobs, and Jack acted like such a dork around her that I decided I didn't want them, especially if they made cool guys turn into complete idiots. At least, that was part of the reason. The other part was because I didn't want to have to wear a bra ever. Kim Talbot had already started wearing one, and Allison and I both agreed it looked way too uncomfortable.

But then, one by one, everyone started to grow boobs—everyone except me, that is—and suddenly I wasn't so against them. But they didn't come and they still haven't come and now I've sort of resigned myself to a lifetime of barely fitted training bras.

I pull the sweatshirt over my head, shimmy out of my jeans, and examine myself in the full-length mirror. The overhead fluorescent lighting is so completely unflattering. I hate how it highlights the slight knobbiness of my knees and the fact that my waist-to-hip ratio is zilch. My eyes travel from my scrawny legs to my curveless trunk, then up past the aforementioned flat chest and on to my head. I sort of like my yard-length hair, even though it's a bland shade of blond, and my superlong eyelashes are cool, too. My mom keeps telling me that any day now, I'll grow out of this awkward phase and my body will catch up to my face, but I don't know.

Mrs. Zeigler bangs on the door and asks me how I look. "Just a minute," I say, quickly stepping into the hundred-and-sixty-dollar (!) gown. I'm surprised to discover it's just a wee bit snug in the hips and waist, and for a split second, I'm hopeful that it'll be snug in other places, too.

But the higher I drag the zipper, the more air comes between me and the satiny material. When it's fully up and locked in place, I realize I could fit my little brother Brody's pet hedgehog into the left cup *alone*.

"Hon?" Mrs. Zeigler starts knocking again. "You okay in there? Need some help?"

Um, yeah. The word "implants" comes to mind.

"Hey, Luce?" I hear Allison call from the other side of the door. "Are you coming out or what?"

After a few minutes that feel like hours, I take a deep breath, turn the lock, and slowly open the door. Both Ally and her mom look a little irritated until they realize I'm drowning in fabric. Then Mrs.

Ziegler's face gets all soft and mushy, like she's watching something on American Movie Classics, and Allison—who's *supposed* to be my best friend—turns the color of red licorice and adjusts the sleeveless bodice of her own perfectly fitted dress.

"You know what?" Mrs. Ziegler asks me, tugging on a pink ribbon rose. "I don't think that *is* your color after all."

Mrs. Ziegler drops me off at home just before dinner. The house smells incredible, filled with the scent of my mother's patented beef stew. I wander into the kitchen and find her chopping vegetables for a salad.

"Did you have a good time?" she asks.

"Mostly."

"What does 'mostly' mean?"

"It means," I say, lifting the lid off the Crock-Pot, "I had a mostly good time, instead of a wholly good one." I reach into the pot and nick a too-hot potato, which burns my fingers so badly I drop it back into the bubbling stew.

"Here," Mom says, handing me a fork. "If you're going to graze, at least do it the right way."

My mom is one of those superwomen who juggles

everything well; she's successful in the workplace (she's a managing photo editor for the *Daily Journal*, the largest newspaper in the state) but never too busy to do things like make dinner from scratch, or take me and Brody to the Franklin Institute to see the latest IMAX movie, or, when he still lived at home, attend every single one of Jack's musical performances.

"So Jack called while you were out."

"What? When?"

"About twenty minutes ago."

It figures. I haven't spoken to my brother in more than a month, since the first day of school, in fact, and he finally calls the one Saturday afternoon I actually have plans.

"What'd he say? Where's he been? Why hasn't he called? When's he coming home?"

Mom laughs. "Why don't you ask him yourself?" she says. "He told me he'd call back for you around six-thirty."

"But that's two whole hours away!"

"You know what would make the time pass faster?"

"What?"

"If you went ahead and set the table."

I walked *right* into that one.

As I collect the necessary dishes and head into the dining room, I start making a mental list of all the things I want to talk to Jack about. His calls have grown so infrequent, I don't want to forget a single thing.

It wasn't always this way. Jack moved to Boston a little over two years ago to study jazz at the world-renowned Berklee College of Music. At first, Jack was always coming home for surprise weekend visits, so I never had to miss him for too terribly long. Lately, though, Jack's obsession with his music has reached an all-time high—which translates into zero visits home and only the occasional phone call.

In some ways, Jack is like this miniature version of my father—he picked up his first instrument, a violin, at the age of three. He was bored with it by the time he turned five and, legend has it, begged my parents to buy him a little person's drum kit. Three years later, he traded drums for piano lessons, and by the time he was ten, he'd already moved on. This go-round, Jack went brass and fell in love with the trumpet, never once looking back.

My dad loves the fact that Jack is some kind of musical prodigy, since music has always been his first love, too. Dad plays saxophone in a jazz combo that tours something like four or five months each year, if you add up all the two-week gigs and random one-nighters. The music gene lies dormant in both me and Brody, a fact that was quickly discovered when my mom, wanting to get extra mileage out of the piano Jack discarded, ordered us to take lessons. The experiment lasted until Brody's first recital, when he somehow managed to butcher "Scarborough Fair" so badly beyond recognition that Mom dismissed our teacher the very next day. The piano still sits, mostly untouched, in the living room, a thin film of dust accumulating on the pretty walnut wood.

Mom calls dinner, and dutifully, the remaining men of the house file in. First my father, clad in his Saturday uniform of tattered jeans and a T-shirt bearing the crest of Delaware University, where he teaches music part-time. Trailing him is Grody Brody, the eleven-year-old bane of my existence and proof, in my humble opinion, that my parents should have stopped procreating after me.

Something you should know about Brody: he eats his boogers. Literally. We can be sitting around the table, chowing down on some baked macaroni and cheese, and he will stick his finger up his nose and pull out a big slimy one. After inspecting said booger for a few seconds, he'll pop the snot ball into his mouth, chew it twice, and swallow, much to my horror and my parents' general lack of interest.

As if that weren't bad enough, the kid sees more action than I do. He's already been sent home from school *six times* this year because Mrs. Laurenger, his sixth-grade teacher, found him making out with Gina Albright behind the climbing wall during recess.

I feel sorry for Gina. If she only knew what goes into that kid's mouth.

We take our regular seats around the table—Dad at the head, me to his left, Mom to his right, and Brody to her right. Jack's seat, the one next to mine, has been empty for the past six months. I think the chair misses Jack, too.

I've barely taken two bites of the stew Mom has ladled into my bowl when Grody Brody starts digging for gold.

"Mom, he's doing it again," I say, dropping my spoon on the table in defeat.

"Doing what?"

"You know. That *thing*."

My dad lifts his head from his own bowl and says, "I thought he stopped doing 'that thing' ages ago."

I roll my eyes at my father, who responds by tossing me a dinner roll. Grody just smiles at my parents, all innocent-like. When he's sure no one's looking, he turns to me and opens his mouth, giving me a sickening view of chewed beef-and-potato.

"Did you see that?" I ask of no one in particular, since no one seems to be paying attention. "How can you even think about eating around that . . . that . . . *thing*?"

"To which thing are you referring?" Dad asks. "Are you talking about '*that* thing,' or just your brother in general?"

"Both."

"That's enough, Lucy," Mom warns, giving me the look. The one moms perfect to make a kid shut up cold, which I do.

"Why are you so cranky, punkin?" Dad asks. "Punkin" is his favorite nickname for me, the one he uses when he's trying to be extra sweet. "I thought you'd be happy that Jack was finally coming home for a visit."

"What?" I say, stunned. "When?"

"He'll be here sometime on Friday," he says. "Just in time for homecoming."

Suddenly, I don't care that Brody's now pillaging his other nostril, or that my mom didn't think to disclose such an important piece of news. In less than a week, Jack will be here, and we'll do all the things we haven't gotten to do for ages, like go to Old New Castle, get some hot dogs from the Cellar Gourmet, and roam around Battery Park. Or maybe I can convince him to take me and Allison down to Dover, home of Delaware's one remaining drive-in movie theater, which I think stays open through Halloween.

"How long will he be here?" I ask. Mom and Dad exchange a weird look. "Well?"

"A little while," Mom says, clearing her throat.

"What, like a four-day weekend?"

"Something like that."

Jack doesn't call until close to seven, which gives me time to start reading *The Scarlet Letter*, which could very well be the most boring book I've ever been assigned to read. I've barely made it through ten pages when the phone rings.

"Hey, Biscuit!" Jack says. "How's high school been treating you?"

"It's okay," I say. It isn't completely a lie. "I have your old French teacher, Madame Aubergine. Ally does, too, but we're not in the same section this year. We both think she's kind of freaky."

"Does she still have that one streak of white hair?"

"Totally!"

"So," Jack says. "What else is new?"

"I should be asking you that," I say.

"Why?"

"Well, where have you been? We haven't heard from you in ages. And the last time I tried to call you there was a message saying your phone had been temporarily disconnected."

"Oh, that," Jack says. "I've been busy, you know,

with school." There's an awkward pause before he continues. "I've also been staying with a friend."

"Really? Why?"

"There were, um, some problems. At my place. But no big deal or anything. . . . Anyway, I didn't call to talk about me. I want to hear about your life. What's going on with you?"

I start to tell him about how weird things have become, how Kim Talbot's now a cheerleader and Kim Tate's no longer her shadow, but after I prattle on for a few minutes with no response from Jack, he says, "Listen, Biscuit—I gotta get going. But I'm coming home on Friday and we can finishing catching up then, okay?"

I'm disappointed—we've only been talking for about seven minutes—but all I say is, "Sure, Jack. That sounds good."

"All righty then."

He hangs up, leaving me with an earful of dial tone and twenty more pages of Hawthorne to go before Family Game Night officially begins.

Since Friday nights belong to friends, Mom insists that we all hang out on Saturday nights. At first, they were Family Movie Nights, but after several unsuccessful trips to the Video King (no one could ever agree on a single flick), we switched to board games: Monopoly, Life, and modified Trivial Pursuit, where

Mom and Dad get the normal questions and Brody and I use the Disney deck.

Before Jack moved to Boston, I loved Family Game Night. Jack has a way of making everything fun. When he's around, he's always cracking jokes and making goofball faces. But ever since he left, things haven't been the same, and lately I've practically had to be dragged kicking and screaming into the den for our weekly dose of enforced family bonding.

I guess I shouldn't complain; after all, I have parents who are still married, and that's more than I can say for most of my friends. Kim Talbot's parents are each on their *third* marriage, and Kim Tate's father's new wife was a senior at Haley High when Jack was a freshman. Even Allison's parents, who were supposedly childhood sweethearts, separated briefly last year when her dad announced that he'd fallen in love with our eighth-grade algebra teacher.

Tonight, Dad pulls out Delawareopoly, the local version of the Milton Bradley classic, and for the first time in ages, I'm happy to play. We keep going until Brody's got two diplomas (aka hotels) on both Old College and Memorial Hall and manages to wipe both Mom and me out in a single round. Then Daddy heads off to the kitchen, where he proceeds to make all four of us clown sundaes—complete with gumball eyes and a sugar-cone hat.

I look at the candy face on my dessert and think, *I have got to get a cooler life*.

The next week creeps by. Allison pesters me night and day about whether or not we're going to the dance, and finally, on Wednesday, I break down and purchase the twelve-dollar ticket. Then, that night, Ally calls to tell me that earlier in the afternoon, Brad Thomas stopped by her locker and asked her to be his date for homecoming. And even though that very morning Allison promised to do my geometry homework for a week if *I* would go to the dance with her, my former best friend tells my former suitor that yes, she'd love to go with *him*.

I listen patiently to her "good news," trying not to lose my temper over the twelve dollars I just wasted. Then she says, "Isn't this perfect, Lucy? Now I can go with Brad like I wanted to, and you can stay home like you wanted to, and everybody gets to be happy!"

I demonstrate my happiness by hanging up.

Then I cry myself to sleep.

# Chapter 3

It's the smell of Mom's famous blueberry pancakes, mixed with scrambled eggs and sausages, that wakes me from my slumber late on Saturday morning. I waited up for Jack until two A.M. before passing out on top of my now tattered copy of *The Scarlet Letter*. Suddenly starving—and eager to see him—I spring from my bed like a kid at Christmas and race downstairs, not even bothering to brush my teeth or hair.

From the green-and-white-tiled hallway, the kitchen looks as it has always looked: warm, buttery, filled with sunflowers and fragrant eucalyptus leaves. Only there's something wrong with this picture. The person behind the fry pan is *not* my mother, clad in her worn weekend bathrobe. Standing where she's supposed to stand is someone much younger, shorter, and bouncier who I've never seen before.

"Hey there," the stranger says, stirring the eggs with one hand and holding back a long, fluffy curtain of auburn curls with the other. "Lucy, right? Can you give me a hand with these? This hair has *got* to go."

Dumbly, I walk to the stove and take the wooden spatula from her. As I stir, she pulls her glossy hair into a messy twist and secures it with a clip. I'm suddenly conscious of my own sleep-crushed coif, which I'm sure looks nowhere near as cute as her wild curls. Even her outfit, which consists of an *X-Files* T-shirt, chalky blue hospital pants, and pink fuzzy bunny slippers, makes me feel underdressed.

"Um, don't take this the wrong way," I say. "But who *are* you?"

"I'm Hannah," she says, reclaiming the spatula. She sticks her nonstirring hand in my face, practically demanding that I shake it. I don't.

"Oh jeez," she says, slapping her forehead. "You must think I'm a real freak. I'm a friend of your brother's. Jack. From school."

"You're from Boston?"

Hannah shakes her head. "God, no. I just go to school there. Actually I grew up in this tiny town in northern California. Blue Lake. Ever hear of it?"

I shake my head.

"Oh, you'd love it," she says. "It's so beautiful, especially in the fall."

I don't say a word. She doesn't notice.

"There are miles and miles of blackberry bushes that nobody owns, and every single Sunday, all summer long, my best friend, Jasmine, and I would pick buckets of berries and turn them into everything from pancakes to fruit pizzas." With that, Hannah clicks off the gas stove, divides the pile of eggs between two plates already filled with pancakes, sets them both on the corner table, and digs in with a gusto that could rival Jack's. "Sit, eat," she says, between mouthfuls. "It's positively scrumptious."

I don't sit. I don't eat. Instead, I say, "Where's my family?"

Hannah laughs. "You say that like I did something with them. Like I've slashed them with a spatula and stashed their mangled bodies in the hall closet or something." I guess I make a weird face because she stops and says, "That was a joke." When I don't respond, she continues, "Abby took Brody to get something for his Halloween costume, and Jack and Michael are over at the school, watching the marching band warm up for the pregame show."

"What? Why didn't he wake me?"

"We ended up catching a ride with some friends heading to Baltimore," Hannah explains. "Got in late last night, or early this morning, depending on how you look at it. He thought you needed your rest. Want some o.j.?" She gets up and starts rifling through our fridge. "Michael gave me the keys to the van. I'll take you over there after breakfast, okay? I'm sure you're dying to see Jack."

The fact that this Hannah person calls my parents by their first names is only slightly less upsetting than the fact that she's been made my chauffeur. The only thing I'm *dying* to do is find out why she's here in the first place. That and why this unexpected piece of luggage is—oh my *god*—drinking her juice from *my* favorite mug.

And then it hits me: she's "a friend." The one Jack's been staying with. The reason he hasn't been home in six months, and most likely the reason he's barely called at all the last several weeks.

The mug-snatching temptress, oblivious to my loathing, helps herself to a second stack of pancakes.

# Chapter 4

"So you're a freshman, right?" Hannah flies through a yellow light at the Hares Corner intersection at about seventy-five miles an hour, kisses her hand, and smacks it on the van's ceiling. "For luck," she says. "So the light won't turn red."

I close my eyes and picture the van hurtling into the back of an egg truck, making the kind of ooey mess that always lands on the front page of the newspaper.

"God, I hated being your age. I mean, I know that's probably *not* what you want to hear, but— Hey, asshole, nice turn signal!" Hannah slams on the breaks, lurching us both forward. "Sorry 'bout that," she says. "So anyway . . . yeah, fourteen. Wow. You're in for about another three years of hell."

"You need to make a left here," I say, gripping the armrest.

"Where?"

"Here," I say. "Here!"

Hannah swerves wildly, nearly taking out two construction barrels in front of the 7-Eleven.

"You know what the worst thing about being fourteen for me was?" she continues without pause. "Fourteen-year-old boys. The testosterone is just *out* of control. Of course, twenty-year-olds aren't much better. I'm still trying to figure out at what age they actually stop being boys and start becoming *men*."

We pull into the parking lot. Hannah, finding no traditional space to her liking, eases the van up onto the grassy hill behind the JV baseball field. When the van stops moving, I bolt, taking off toward the brass section.

"Hey, wait up!" Hannah calls from behind.

I ignore her, even though I know it's a crappy thing to do, and continue to tear ahead, pushing through a small group of seniors sneaking beers by the far side of the fence. I spot the back of Jack's black leather jacket up ahead. He's standing with a couple of familiar-looking guys eating hot dogs, and because he can't see me, I decide to give him a surprise piggyback. After a running leap, I wrap my arms around him for balance and say, "You could've woken me up, dork!"

"I didn't know I was supposed to," replies the victim, who doesn't sound at all like my brother. The two other guys, the ones I thought looked so familiar, are starting to look a little *more* familiar—like some of the juniors and seniors I've seen around Haley. They snicker as I slowly lower myself to the ground, hoping—praying—that my ears have betrayed me and this really *is* Jack.

It's not.

"I thought you were someone else," I say flatly, by way of an apology. I try not to stare at his *Baywatch*-blond hair, focusing instead on a patch of seemingly poreless skin.

"That's okay," he says, his green eyes peering at me through the chunky black frames of his retro glasses. "There are worse things than having a pretty girl jump you in broad daylight."

His friends snicker some more, and even though I know the comment was made for their benefit, I start to blush. It's not every day a cute older boy refers to me as "pretty."

Then I hear it. Anyone in an eight-mile radius could've heard it.

"Hey, Biscuit!" Jack bellows from far off, jumping around and waving his arms. "Over here!"

The stranger nudges me. "I think you're being paged."

I nod weakly, my face hot enough to light a fireplace full of wet wood. Then I turn and walk toward my soon-to-be-murdered older brother, who's still flailing his limbs around in various directions. Under normal circumstances I'd probably be turning cart-wheels. Yet something—or *someone*—who may or may not be watching me walk away keeps me in a reserved state.

But as Jack races toward me, my embarrassment begins to melt away. He swoops me up into his arms, twirls me around a few times, then places me gently back on the ground. "Look at you," he says, shaking his head. "I feel like I haven't seen you in a year."

I punch him lightly on the arm. "Yeah, well, no one asked you to stay away so long."

"Oh, so that's how it's gonna be, huh?" Jack lifts his hands into two fists and starts circling me. "Wanna fight about it?"

I rise to the challenge. "You want a piece of me?" I say, squinting and trying to look tough. I take a few loose jabs, hitting nothing but air, then aim right for the gut. Jack lets this punch just graze his stomach before he jumps back, clutches his middle, and cries, "Oof!"

"Faker," I say. "What, are you too chicken to fight for real?"

"That does it," Jack growls, shedding his jacket and dropping it right on the grass. "Let's get it on."

I'm bracing myself for battle when the *Baywatch* boy walks by. My arms drop to my sides. Jack reaches forward, musses my hair, and says, "Whatsa matter, Biscuit? You all talk?"

"Quit it," I say, pushing his hand away.

Cute Boy and his buddies have passed, but Cute Boy alone is looking back at me. I squirm under his gaze, not sure if I should smile or look away. Before I can decide, Jack tackles me. I land on my side, half my face pressing into the moist ground.

"*Get off of me!*" I holler, wriggling out from under him. Cute Boy has disappeared. My jeans feel damp; when I look down, I see they're crusted with dirt and leaf bits. "Look what you did!"

Hannah approaches, holding her rust-colored corduroy jacket tightly closed. "Hey, you two," she says. "Lost you there for a second."

I scowl. Too bad we didn't lose her completely.

Jack kisses her hello, not a peck on the cheek but a full on, let-me-introduce-my-tongue-to-yours kiss. *Gag.* I look away, wiping ground gunk off my chin and pretending to be really interested in the alumni association's face-painting booth. "Stop," Hannah says teasingly. "You're making your sister uncomfortable."

"Aw, Lucy doesn't care," Jack says. "Right, Biscuit?"

"Can we go sit down?" I ask a little too loudly. "The game's about to start."

Jack checks his watch. "Yeah, in like twenty minutes."

"But I want to get a good seat." I wince; even I could hear the whine in that sentence.

"All right," he says. He takes Hannah's hand in his. "So we'll go nab some prime bleacher space. Just relax, okay?"

"Whatever," I say, brushing past the happy couple. They don't seem to mind.

At halftime, Jack brings me a peace offering of nachos and once-hot chocolate—not the tastiest combination, but since I turned down Hannah's breakfast hours earlier, I'm close to starving and can't really refuse. As I shove the gluey cheese-covered chips into my half-frozen mouth, Jack huddles closer to me and whispers, "Don't be mad, Luce. I was just psyched to see you. I didn't mean to get you all dirty."

"Well, duh," I say, nudging him with my shoulder. "But Jack—did you have to call me *Biscuit*?"

Jack frowns slightly. "I thought you liked it when I called you that."

"I do, but . . ."

"Not in front of hottie guys," Hannah pipes up. She flashes me one of those smiles, like just because we both have ovaries we're on the same level. I ignore her, pretending to be really into the halftime show.

"Hey," Jack says suddenly, pointing to the sprightly blonde on the top of the cheerleader pyramid. "Isn't that Kim Tate?"

"Talbot. Kim Talbot."

"Whatever. I can't believe you're friends with a *cheerleader*." He says this last word with the same inflection I normally reserve for Brody.

"I told you, we're not really friends anymore."

" 'Cause she's a cheerleader?"

"No," I say patiently. "Because she's turned into an elitist airhead."

I start giggling and Jack joins in. It feels good, sitting here with my brother, being silly, like he hasn't been gone at all. Until *she* interrupts, that is.

"You know, J," she says, in this gross, naughty-girl voice. "I used to be a cheerleader."

"Oh, yeah?" Jack grins. "Did you have a skirt like that?" Hannah nods, placing both of her hands on his left knee. Jack leans into her puffball of curls and says, "Do you still have it?"

"Hey, Jack," I say, purposely interrupting their cheese-fest. "You think I could get another hot chocolate?"

"Sorry, Biscuit. I'm out of cash."

Hannah reaches into her Pee Wee Herman lunch box of a purse and pulls out a five-dollar bill.

"Here," she says. "This round's on me."

I look at the money. No way am I accepting her charity. "You know what?" I say, pasting on a faux smile. "I really shouldn't have a second cup. Gotta watch that figure." I pat my stomach for emphasis.

Jack frowns. "Since when do you worry about your weight?"

"You miss a lot of things when you don't come home for six months," I say.

Hannah places the money back in her wallet, her cheerful face finally falling slightly. This, I have to admit, is deeply satisfying.

The visiting team's marching band finishes their routine, an uninspired tribute to the musicals of Andrew Lloyd Webber, which even *I* know is passé. "Jesus, do these guys *suck*," Jack says. Then he turns to me. "So where's the rest of the old gang anyway?"

"Well, Allison's mom made her go with her to this stupid dog show in Lancaster, and they won't be back until three or so."

"Allison is Lucy's best friend," Jack informs Hannah, who nods like she's taking mental notes.

"And what about Kim Number Two?"

I shrug. "She's probably around here somewhere. Maybe under the bleachers, making out with her cool new boyfriend. Besides, I told you, I don't really hang out with her anymore."

I must sound really bitter or something, because

Jack and Hannah exchange a look. Like I need them to telepathically signal to each other just how pitiful I am.

This is not how I pictured things. Sitting here with the two of them makes me feel itchy inside. It makes me feel like I don't belong. I stick it out until right before halftime, then decide to bolt.

"Oh, look!" I point off into the distance. "I see Tabitha," I say, even though I don't. "I think I'll go hang with her for a while." I wait a few seconds for Jack to protest, and when he doesn't, I slink off. The Haley band is tuning up; if I know Jack, he'll be too engrossed in their big show to even notice I'm gone.

I look around to see if there's anyone else I can sit with, but I don't spot a single familiar face—not even Cute Boy's. Hanging with my dad at the alumni booth is too embarrassing an option. Instead, I sneak behind the wall of Porta-Potties and hide until the last five minutes of the game, trying not to feel like the loser I am.

# Chapter 5

After the Chelsea Chargers trounce our Comets 21 to 3, no one feels much like doing anything, so we (thankfully) decide to head home. For a minute I think maybe Jack and I can sneak in some quality brother-sister bonding time, but he asks Dad for the van so he can show Hannah Battery Park. *Our* park. I end up riding shotgun in Dad's ancient Volvo while Jack and his new girlfriend speed off in the opposite direction.

Dad lets me pout in silence for most of the ride. Then he says, "Let's stop at the Charcoal Pit." The Pit makes the best hamburgers in the entire state, if not the entire world, with just the right amount of grease broiled in. "Sounds good," I say, and I think I actually mean it.

The place is fairly empty for a Saturday, and as Dad puts in our orders—cheeseburger, onion rings, and black-and-white malted for me; double bacon burger, vinegar fries, and a root beer for him—I sit down at our favorite table, a real high one pushed up against the window. When I was younger, and Mom was still working nights and weekends at the paper, and Dad hadn't started touring again, this was our place. Every Sunday, after a matinee at the Regal, Dad, Jack, Brody, and me would come to the Pit and sit at this table, watching the cars stream down Concord Pike in rainbow blurs. We'd order too much food and eat off each other's soggy paper plates, and eventually Jack would coax Brody into a burping contest, and even though they were being gross, those were the times I loved them best, including the booger eater.

But once Jack got his license *and* Echo Erhard, he spent more and more time away from home. Then Mom got promoted and didn't have to work weekends anymore, and Dad decided it was time to get the band back together. And Sundays stopped being Sundays, and that was that.

"So what do you think?" Dad asks.

"About what?"

"Hannah."

"Oh," I say. *"Her."*

"Yes, *'her.' "*

"I don't know," I say. "I guess I don't think she's all that, even though *she* certainly does."

Dad chuckles.

"What's so funny?"

"You," he says. "Do you remember what you thought of Echo Erhard when you first met her?"

I shrug.

36

"Come on, Luce. You *hated* her. You antagonized her constantly. And then two months later you were begging her to braid your hair and take you out for ice cream."

"That," I say, waving my hand dismissively, "was an entirely different matter."

"Yeah," Dad says. "It was."

"Hey! Wait a second—did you know about her?"

"Who, Echo?"

"No, *Father*. Hannah. Did you know she was coming home with Jack? That she even existed?"

"Oh, look," Dad says. "I think that's our food."

The waitress places my Pit Deluxe in front of me, and it smells so good that I don't have the willpower to rail into Dad for avoiding my question. Instead, I bite into my burger—and promptly make a face at the total lack of juice. "Ugh," I say. "It's too cooked."

"Let me see."

Dad takes a bite of his own burger and makes a similar face. He hails the waitress back to our table. "Excuse me, miss, but we ordered these medium rare."

"No can do," she says. "Health codes. Gotta be cooked well or not cooked at all."

I know it's stupid, but suddenly I feel really old. It wasn't all that long ago we ate our burgers bloody. Or was it? Now Jack's off at college, and Brody can't seem to keep his eleven-year-old hands off Gina Albright, and the small surge of excitement I had when I first got my period wore off at least four months ago.

"Dad?" I say, pushing my plate away. "Can we get this to go? I don't think I feel so good."

"Aw, Luce," he says, kissing me on my forehead. "Go ahead and leave it. I'm sure Mom's got dinner waiting for us anyway."

We slide out of our seats, and he looks at me like he knows it's not overcooked cow that's making me feel ill. So I hug him, more tightly than I have in a long, long time.

We reach the house just before five; Jack and Hannah don't roll in for four more hours. When they arrive, we Doyles—minus the Brodster, who has holed himself up in the basement with the newest installation in Sega's Final Fantasy series—have just finished watching *Carrie*, this freaky movie about a girl who gets showered in pig's blood at her senior prom. The video is a consolation prize from my mother, who thought it might make me feel like less of a loser for spending my first homecoming sandwiched between her and my dad on our battered plaid couch instead of on a dance floor with someone like Cute Boy. She doesn't say this, of course, but I'm not *completely* clueless.

"Forget the way home?" Dad jokes as the hand-holding duo enters the family room.

"Something like that," Jack says. He gives me a funny look. "What are you doing here? Didn't the dance start hours ago?"

"Dances," I sigh, with as much dignity as I can muster, "are stupid wastes of time."

"Couldn't find a date, huh?" Jack grins like it's a joke, but my silence—everyone's pin-drop silence—makes him realize he's right. His grin melts away; I fly from the couch, race up the stairs, and lock myself in the guest bathroom, where I promptly burst into tears.

After a minute or so, there's a timid knock on the door. It's Jack. "Luce?" he says softly. "Lucy, I'm sorry. I didn't know. C'mon out, Luce. Let me make it up to you. Let's go have some real fun."

"Leave me alone!" I splurt through a thunderstorm of tears. "Go back to Boston! And take your stupid big-haired girlfriend with you!"

Jack's voice loses some of its softness. "Hey now," he says. "Keep it down. She's not deaf, you know."

"Like I care!" In a flash, I'm off my toilet perch, yanking the door wide open. "I mean it, Jack! I didn't think anything could make this day worse, but then you come home and— You. You! Of all people. So just leave. Take your stuff and go!" I put my hands on his chest and roughly shove him away. Jack just stands there, eyes wide, shocked by my behavior—which, I must admit, has shocked even me.

"I can't believe this," he says slowly. "You're mad at *me?*"

I wipe a yo-yo of snot from my reddened nose. "You didn't even come home for my birthday. And now, *finally,* you're here . . . but with *her* . . . and you didn't wake me up and she almost killed us on the way to Haley . . . and . . . and . . ." I pause, my breath jiggling in my chest and throat like a little earthquake.

"And what?" Jack's eyes are on fire, and I shrink under his stare. "You're pissed off because I went to college and got a girlfriend? Jesus, Lucy. Grow up."

His harsh tone cuts me wide open. "I wish you'd just leave again," I say, weakly pushing him farther away. "Just go."

Jack clucks his tongue and shakes his head at me in mock sadness. "Too bad you feel that way, because my 'big-haired girlfriend' just happens to be your new roommate." He starts walking back downstairs, still shaking his head.

"What's that supposed to mean?"

"It means," Jack says, gripping the handrail, "this is more than a random weekend visit. Mom and Dad gave us the okay last night. Hannah and I are moving in."

# Chapter 6

It takes a few seconds for Jack's revelation to sink in before I tear down the steps after him. "What do you mean, 'moving in'?" I holler from the first-floor landing. Jack slams the door to his basement bedroom in response.

"Hey!" My mother comes out of the kitchen, drying her hands on a dish towel. "What's all the noise about?"

"Is it true? Are they moving in?"

My mother sighs. "I was hoping we could talk about this tomorrow after church."

"Church? We don't go to church."

"Well, maybe we should start!" she snaps, throwing the towel down for emphasis. My mother, the even-tempered saint. I look at her in disbelief.

"Come," she commands, returning to the kitchen. I follow. "Sit," she says. I do. She takes a seat next to me, sucks in a deep breath, and says—nothing.

"Mom?" I say after a few minutes.

"All right, Luce. Here's the deal." She drums her fingers on the table, then crosses one arm over the other. "Jack's going through some tough stuff right now, and he needs a little time off. To think. To make plans. So, yes, he's moving back in. For a little while, anyway."

"What do you mean by 'tough stuff'? Is he okay?"

"He's fine, Lucy. It's just . . . complicated."

"Complicated how? Why are you being so vague?"

Mom sighs lightly. "I'm not trying to be."

"But what about school? What's Jack going to do about school?"

"I don't know."

"And what about the girl—why does *she* have to be here?"

"Because Hannah's part of the package . . . for now."

"What's that supposed to mean?"

"It means," Mom says slowly, "that they're together. And that they're going to be together here."

"I still don't understand why she has to move into my room."

"Aw, Luce." Mom reaches for my hand. "We just thought . . . since you have that extra bed . . . It seemed like the best solution."

"Why can't she stay in Jack's room? I mean, they're *obviously* sleeping together." She shoots me a sharp glance. "Come on, Mother. They were living together, weren't they?"

"That's not the point," she says. "I don't think it's appropriate, that's all."

I plead, "Isn't there any way around this?"

"Think of it this way—you always wanted a sister."

I roll my eyes. "I meant instead of Brody."

Mom pats my hand, then rises. "Well, no one's moving into anybody's room right now. Hannah can sleep on the pullout in the den tonight. Okay?" She kisses me on the top of my head. "This old lady needs to get herself to bed. And you look pretty exhausted too, missy."

"One more question?"

"What?" She leans her head against the doorway.

"Do we really have to start going to church?"

"We'll see."

I try to fall asleep, but my brain can't wrap itself around the day's events. First Jack shows up out of nowhere with some annoying ex-cheerleading chick he's shacking up with, and now this. Dropping out of school. Moving back home.

Funny how a week ago, I couldn't wait for Jack to come home, and now that he's here, all I want is for him to go far, far away.

Due to a wicked emotional hangover, I spend most of Sunday in bed, watching a *Real World* marathon on MTV under a mountain of blankets, waiting for a call from Allison that never comes. Periodically, I hear footsteps in the hallway and brace myself, thinking it's Mom coming to ask if I'm okay, or Dad coming to see if I'm hungry, or Hannah coming to invade my space, or even Jack coming to fix things between us.

No one comes.

# Chapter 7

At school the next morning, I wait for Allison outside her homeroom. "So how was it?" I ask when she arrives two minutes before first bell.

"How was what?"

"The dance."

"Oh, that." Allison looks at her black suede sneakers. "It was okay."

"Just okay?"

Allison nods, then says, "Look, I gotta go over my French vocab. Madame Aubergine's making us learn about some ancient tribe of African storytellers, the Grinches or something."

"Griots," I say, but she's already halfway through the door.

I can't believe she blew me off. It's bad enough she didn't call this weekend. But to act like I barely exist after going on a single date—with Brad Thomas, no less—makes her worse than the Kims.

I wonder if I'm about to lose another friend.

Speak of the devil, or devils, as the case may be. Two seconds later I'm bombarded by the Kims, who stop me outside the girls' bathroom on 2 West.

"Is it true?" Kim Tate says, grabbing my wrist.

"Is what true?"

Kim Talbot smiles sweetly. "We heard your brother's home."

"Which one?"

"C'mon, Luce," Kim Tate says impatiently.

I confirm the rumor, and the Kims trade looks of what could only be described as pure joy. For as long as I can remember, every friend I've ever invited over has developed a crush on Jack. Usually, it doesn't bother me—if anything, I sort of like it that my brother is so crush-worthy. But today it makes me want to barf.

"So, Lucy," Kim Talbot says smoothly, linking her arm through mine. "We were thinking the five of us should get together this weekend. Like a slumber party or something. The old gang."

"Yeah," the other Kim adds, switching her twenty-pound book bag to her other shoulder. "Think your mom would let us have it at your place?"

I blink a few times. They've acted like I'm practically invisible since school started, and now they're suddenly my best friends again? All for the mere possibility of being in close proximity to my brother?

"No way," I say coldly.

Now it's their turn to do the blinking.

"Are you sure?" Kim Talbot asks. "Your mom used to love to have us over."

"Yeah," Kim Tate echoes. "Maybe you should ask her first."

The warning bell rings.

"Sorry," I say. "The house is getting kind of crowded." I start to walk away, feeling their angry eyes burn holes in my back. I hear one of them mutter, "What's that supposed to mean?" and I can't help myself. I stop, turn around slowly, and say, "Guess you didn't get the whole story. Jack brought home his *girlfriend*. They're living together now."

Their jaws drop at about the same moment, but I don't have time to savor the effect. I've got less than a minute to get to Mr. Bentley's algebra class. The man is a monster. If you're not inside that room when the final bell rings, you're locked out. Then not only do you get a zero for attendance that day, you have to find a place to hide from patrolling administrators, all of whom are overly eager to give you detention.

Once I'm sure the Kims can no longer see me, I sprint off toward the east wing. My school's the largest in the state—two floors, each stretching over a quarter of a mile from end to end—and it's hard enough getting from class to class in the allotted three minutes when I haven't made any pit stops. Of course, it's even harder to get somewhere when you're not really paying attention to where you're going and you slip on a carelessly discarded No. 2 pencil, go *flying* across the grimy linoleum floor, and end up in a tangle of limbs and backpack straps in front of at least a dozen people.

"Hey, are you okay?" A large paw of a hand swoops in front of my face. It takes me a few seconds to realize I'm being offered assistance. "Thanks," I say, using the paw to pull myself up. It's not until a few seconds after *that* that I realize just whose paw it is.

"I know you," says the cute older boy from the football game. "It's Biscuit, right?"

"Um, a-actually," I stammer, "it's Lucy. Biscuit's just a nickname."

"It's cute," he says. "Suits you."

My ears burn at these words. Then the bell rings, and I blush a different kind of hot.

"I'm sorry," I say, practically whispering.

"What for?"

"For making you late."

He shakes his head, and says, "Nah, don't worry about it. It's only chem lab. Foster'll be too busy handing out goggles to notice I'm gone." He smiles then, revealing a deep, adorable dimple where the right side of his mouth meets the bottom of his cheek, like half of a pair of facial parentheses. He reaches out and brushes something from my hair.

"Leaf," he says, showing me the tiny burst of fall and then tossing it aside. I fight the urge to snatch it as a souvenir for my memory box and grab my back-pack instead.

"Tobin Scacheri," booms Vice Principal Sherman from behind me. "Where are you supposed to be right now?"

Tobin (!) takes me by the elbow and says, "Chem lab. But this girl here—Lucy—she's hurt, Mr. Sherman. I gotta get her to the nurse's office."

"Hurt?"

"Ankle," Tobin says, squeezing my elbow. Instinctively, I let my left foot roll over to the side a bit and say, "Ow."

"What happened?" Sherman asks, stifling a yawn.

"Slipped on a pencil," I say, limping toward him a bit. Sherman's eyes narrow to thin slits, but he lets us go anyway. Tobin lifts my arm and slips it around his neck so I can "lean" on him for support. I don't exactly object.

"You were great," Tobin whispers as we slowly shuffle down the long hall. "Very convincing."

"Actually," I say, "my ankle *does* sort of hurt." Which is totally a lie, but Tobin Scacheri's shoulder feels so nice against my temple that I'm not ready to let it go just yet.

After dutifully delivering me to the nurse's office and picking up an official late pass, Tobin takes off. At first, I'm disappointed that he doesn't say goodbye.

But then his face reappears in a small window. He gives me a quick wave, and before he dips out of sight again, I'm rewarded with another flash of dimple.

Oh *wow*.

When I get on the bus to go home after school, I find Tabitha Donnelly sitting in the seat we used to share up until this year, when Tabitha decided she was too cool to ride with the rest of us.

"Hey," she says, scooting closer to the window. Which I suppose is her way of asking me to sit with her. Which I do, of course, because it would be too awkward not to.

"So," I say, eyeing her lime green fishnet tights. "How's it going?"

"It's going," she sighs. "It's going, going, *gone*." Tabitha picks at the ends of her supershort fuchsia hair, rubbing them between her thumb and forefinger. I'm not quite sure how to respond to that, so I don't, and that's basically all we say to each other during the six-minute ride to her stop.

But when the bus screeches to a halt across the street from Tabitha's town house, she doesn't move. "Um, isn't this your stop?" I ask her.

"Oh, right," she says, still not moving.

"Are you okay?" I ask. "You look really out of it."

Tabitha suddenly snaps to attention. "Now you care?"

"Never mind," I mumble, staring at my lap. The bus lurches forward, and as I contemplate switching seats, I feel Tabitha's hand on my arm.

"I'm sorry," she says. "I shouldn't have barked at you."

"Whatever."

The bus reaches my stop next, and I bolt. I'm halfway down the block before I hear Tabitha yell, "Jesus, Lucy, will you slow down a little?"

I seem to be hearing that a lot lately.

"Thank you," Tabitha says after I've allowed her to catch up. "You don't know how hard it is to jog in platforms."

We walk in silence until we reach the end of my driveway. Then I say, "What's up with you, Tabitha? You've been MIA since August, and then you get mad at me for asking how you are. That's so wrong. I'm not the one who did the ditching, remember?"

Tabitha's chin quivers slightly. I can't even remember the last time I saw her cry. Probably not since the day Buddy Boyer pantsed her in fourth-grade gym class and everyone saw her naked butt as she ran back into the locker room.

Sympathy gets the best of me. "Do you want to talk or something?"

She stares at my chin, still trying not to cry, then nods.

"It's cold," I say, motioning toward the door. "Let's go inside."

# Chapter 8

We head into the kitchen. Tabitha shakes off her coat and drapes it across the back of her chair before sitting down and crossing her legs daintily at the ankles. From the look on her face I can tell this is going to be a Cocoa Conversation. In our group—well, in our former group—talking over cocoa was standard when any of us entered crisis mode. The number of marshmallows added to said cocoa indicated the level of seriousness attached to said crisis. Without a word, I begin to fill the kettle.

"How many?" I ask, pulling an unopened bag of marshmallows from the cereal cabinet.

"Three," Tabitha says. "No, four. Actually, let's go for five."

Whoa. The last time Tab called for a five-alarm cocoa was when her mom announced that Tab's second stepfather was not only cheating on her, but was doing so with another guy. Still, even that wasn't so bad because she (the soon-to-be former Mrs. Donnelly-Steed-Bernstein) had already fallen madly in love with Nunzio, the pastry chef who designed the cake for her third wedding.

I scoop mad amounts of Swiss Miss mix into two cappuccino-sized bowl-mugs, fill them only halfway with the steaming water, stir extensively, and dump a whole fistful of fat marshmallows over the tops. Tabitha takes a swig of hers before even placing the mug on the table, promptly burning her tongue and causing her to sprout tears.

"Tabitha, talk to me. What's wrong? Is Nunzio—I mean, is he . . . *you know* . . . too?"

She sniffles. "No. God, no. He's a total shithead, but straight as a ruler."

"Then what?"

"It's Elliot," she says, chin quivering. "Well, Elliot and me. And . . . um . . . what happened."

"Tabitha," I say. "Speak English."

She sighs and swallows some more cocoa. "So last month Elliot and I talked practically every night. For hours. And then the phone bill came, and it was kind of massive."

"How massive?"

"Two hundred bucks' worth of massive."

"Oh."

"Yeah," she says, scooping out a half-melted marshmallow with her lime green pinkie nail and transferring it into her mouth. "So this was a big deal, you know? And then Nunzio *flipped*. Wanted to know why we were talking so much, what we talked about.

"And then," she continues, "he found it."

"What?"

"This poem. *The* poem. Elliot wrote it for me after the night I let him . . . you know. Touch me. *There*."

"Oh."

Tabitha gives me a sort of squinty look. "Is this okay? Me talking to you about this kind of stuff?"

"Sure," I say. "Why wouldn't it be?"

"I don't know." She takes another sip of cocoa. "Anyway, Nunzio freaked. And then my mom freaked. They both started calling me these horrible names. Telling me I was turning into some kind of slut. So I called Lizzie and begged her to send me a train ticket, so I could get away for the weekend. This was last weekend."

"Oh."

I think if I say "oh" one more time, I'm going to have to strangle myself for being such a complete and utter lame-*oh*.

"I didn't tell them I was going. I just took off. I had to see Elliot." Tabitha's slender hands are clasped tightly around her mug. The blood has drained from her knuckles, she's holding on so tight. "It's hard to explain, Lucy. I guess it's like . . . it's like my whole life is this gigantic ball of fake. But when I'm with him, and he's giving me that look, or touching my cheek with the back of his finger . . . God, Lucy, *that's* what feels real. That's my reality. You know?"

*That's just it*, I think. *I* don't.

"He was so happy to see me," she says. "I helped him clean out the cappuccino machines after the café closed. And then we went upstairs to the break room and talked for hours. Then he kissed me, and it was weird for a minute but then it wasn't, and his hands were just everywhere. And then we . . . we started to . . . and it felt so good, Lucy. I mean, *so good*. Elliot kept asking me if I wanted to stop. But I didn't. I didn't want it to stop at all."

Tabitha starts to cry again, quietly at first and then a little louder. After a while she doesn't even bother to wipe away the fat tears racing down her cheeks.

"What if Nunzio's right?" she says. "What if I am a slut?"

I get the feeling she wants me to tell her she's not, and I don't know, maybe she isn't. But it scares me, the way she talks about it, like it was an accident. Like me slipping on that pencil. How do you *accidentally* have sex with a person?

"Well," I say. "Do you feel like a slut?"

Tabitha shakes her head. "No. That's just it. I wanted to do it as much as he did. And it was so . . . *nice*." She sighs. "How could something so nice make me a bad person?"

I don't answer, because I don't know what I'm supposed to say. I don't even know what I *want* to say, really.

"Tell me I can trust you, Lucy," Tabitha whispers hoarsely. "Tell me you're not like the rest of them. They'd think I was a slut, too. But you—you can't be like that. Okay?"

"Of course," I say.

"Promise me," she says, reaching out and grabbing my hand. "You won't tell *anybody*, not even Ally."

"I promise." I look at Tab's face, all red and puffy. She looks so scared that I feel scared for her, but the only thing I can do is hug her. She hugs me back, really hard, and then she starts crying again and gets the right sleeve of my sweatshirt all soppy.

After a while, Tab calms down some. "Sorry about your shirt," she sniffs.

"It's okay," I say. "That's what friends are for, right?"

She smiles a little, and her hunched-up shoulders relax a bit. "I'm really glad you said that, Lucy. It's funny, because on the bus, you made it sound like I'd been ignoring you. But I've felt like *you* were the one ignoring *me*. Ever since Ally's party . . . I guess I thought you didn't want to be friends with the kind of girl who lets herself get felt up on the third date."

It's hard to describe how this last part makes me feel. Because even though it kind of creeps me out that someone my age has had *actual* sex with another human being, I can't really judge her. Because who knows what I would do if some hot poet boy tried to put his hands up my skirt? Or Tobin Scacheri—what if *he* tried to touch me there? I think how good his shoulder felt supporting my head, and that was just his *shoulder*.

"I should go," Tabitha says. "My mom's gonna go ballistic if I'm not there when she gets home. She'll think I ran away to my sister's again. Or something."

I wonder if the soon-to-be Mrs. Nunzio realizes how much of an "or something" there is for her to worry about, but I don't dare say this out loud. Instead, I walk Tab to the door. "Call me if you need anything," I say. I hug her again, so she knows I really mean it, and she says okay and then she is gone.

I spend the rest of the afternoon alone in my room, thinking of Tabitha. It's strange; for so long, I desperately wanted something—anything—to happen, and now it has, only not to me. Suddenly my Tobin Scacheri story doesn't seem all that important in comparison.

Just when there's a glimmer of hope that I might actually catch up to everybody else, they leave me even farther behind.

# Chapter 9

Allison calls during dinner and my mother tells her I'll call her back later. It's not like I'm eating anything. My appetite's just *gone*. Earlier I asked Jack to pass the pepper and he acted like he didn't hear me, even though I know he did. I kept asking until Dad took mercy on me, reached over, and passed it to me himself. So here I sit, making racetracks in a hill of mashed potatoes with my fork, then herding stray peas to the starting gate. Hannah, on the other hand, has already cleaned her plate once and is starting on seconds.

Finally, my mother declares the meal officially over and I escape to the sanctuary that is my room. Allison answers on the first ring.

"I can't believe you didn't tell me!" she squeals, without any sort of greeting. Her normally soprano voice has somehow managed to hit the high pitch of a Mariah Carey ballad.

"Tell you what?" I swallow hard, wondering how Tabitha's news could've gotten out so quickly.

"You know."

I'm quiet for a minute, frantically searching my

brain for some plausible way to get out of this mess, which isn't easy when you're as horrible a liar as I am.

"Oh, give it up, Lu-cy," she says, drawing out the syllables of my name. "Kim Talbot told me all about it during study hall. How could you let me hear it from her?"

A lightbulb clicks on over my head and I realize she's talking about Jack, not Tab. I let out a stomach full of air and say, "I didn't think it was that big a deal. I mean, it's not like he's *your* brother."

"I don't care whose brother he is! You're supposed to tell your friends these things. Especially your *best* friend."

"So, what?" I ask. "Should I have flashed the Bat signal the minute Jack stepped through the door?"

"What are you *talking* about?" Allison practically screeches. I pull the phone from my ear and try to shake away the ringing sensation her excited shrieks have caused. "I meant about Tobin Scacheri!"

"Huh?" I say, unable to make the connection. "What does any of this have to do with Tobin Scacheri?"

"Lucy!" Allison shouts. *"It's all about Tobin Scacheri!"*

After she settles down some, Ally explains the whole thing. Apparently, Lori Pfefferminz saw me walking down the hall with Tobin Scacheri's arm around my shoulder and felt all wounded because Lori's had the hugest crush on him since last spring. Then Lori started sobbing about how Tobin was falling all over some *freshman* to her cheerleader friends, and one of them just happened to be Kim Talbot. Then Kim tracked Allison down to confirm the rumor, only Ally couldn't because she didn't even know that I knew Tobin Scacheri, let alone that I was *dating* him.

"We're not dating," I say. "I barely even know the guy."

"Then why was he carrying you down the hallway?"

"Allison, he was helping me to the nurse's office. I slipped on the floor right in front of him, then the bell rang and—"

"And he rescued you!" she sighs. "How *romantic*."

"Oh, yeah," I say sarcastically. "Klutziness is such a turn-on."

I tell her about our first encounter at the homecoming game, but instead of laughing, Ally sighs again and says, "You're so lucky, Lucy."

"Lucky?" I echo. "Tobin Scacheri hardly even knows I'm alive. At least you had a date for homecoming." I begin to chew on a twisted loop of phone cord.

"Ha! Some date. I should've stayed home with you."

"Why?" The cord drops from my mouth. "What happened?"

"Can I just tell you, Lucy," she says. "You were right about Brad Thomas. He acted like such a dork. First he kept throwing M&M's down the front of my dress, like my boobs were goalposts or something. Then he kept trying to snap my bra, only I was wearing a strapless, so all he did was make the hooks pop open. And after all this, when he took me home, he *still* tried to kiss me, tongue and everything, even though his mom was sitting right there in the front seat."

"Oh, Ally," I say, stifling a giggle. "That's *terrible*."

"Tell me about it."

We don't dwell on her misery for long, as Allison is eager to steer talk back to me and Tobin.

"Maybe he likes you, Luce," she bubbles. "Do you think he likes you?"

I feel myself start to blush. "I told you—I barely know him."

"Yeah, but maybe," she says, "it's your cosmic destiny or something. Maybe that's why you keep doing stupid things around him. Because karma works like that, you know. I mean, if you two are meant to be together, the universe will do anything in its power to help make it happen."

If that's the case, I wish the universe would let me keep at least a *smidge* of dignity. How many times can

I make a total idiot of myself in front of a cute junior boy before he writes me off as a silly freshman geek?

There's a soft knock on the door.

"Hold on a sec," I say. After covering the mouthpiece I yell, "Come in."

It's Hannah. Over one shoulder is a worn camouflage knapsack. The opposite hand holds a giant red plastic suitcase.

"Is this a bad time?" she asks quietly. She looks tired.

"No," I say. "It's fine." It's not fine, of course, but it's also inevitable.

When I put the receiver back up to my ear, I hear Allison chattering away. "Lucy? What's going on? Who is it? Luce?"

"I have to go," I tell her. "I'll talk to you tomorrow." I hang up before she has the chance to object.

Hannah smiles slightly, dragging the monster suitcase over to the spare daybed. I watch her struggle to lift it up, wondering why my strapping big brother isn't here to help her.

"It's amazing," she grunts, "how much a few pairs of shoes can weigh."

As Hannah unpacks, I generously begin to clear out a couple of dresser drawers. She doesn't seem to notice. Instead, she tosses her clothes on the bed in small piles that quickly grow into great big heaps.

Indian-print scarves, chenille sweaters, and at least a half a dozen pairs of jeans in as many different colors spill over to the floor, falling like a fabric snowstorm on top of Shoe Mountain. No wonder the suitcase was so heavy. I could surrender my entire dresser, the closet, *and* the surface of my bed and she *still* couldn't fit that wardrobe into my room.

"Don't worry," Hannah says, as if she's read my mind. "I'm not keeping all of this up here. Jack's making some space in the basement, too."

"Do you, um, want me to help carry anything downstairs?"

"Thanks," she says, fingering a plush shirt in deep plum. "Maybe later. I need to sort this mess out first." Hannah brings one of the sleeves up to her nose, rubs the soft velvet against her cheek. "Mmm. I *love* this shirt. It always feels so . . . so . . . yummy. You know? It's impossible to feel crappy when you're wearing velvet." She lets the shirt drop to the bed. Then, without even turning away, she proceeds to tear off her thermal underwear top. I'm so shocked by her complete lack of self-consciousness that I forget to look away. It's strange, seeing her standing there half naked, with the tops of her breasts rising from a zebra-striped satin bra. She doesn't even try to cover herself up like my friends and I do in the locker room after gym class.

"There," Hannah says, smoothing the front of the "yummy" shirt. "That's *much* better."

It's at this point I realize I have two options: I can sit here and watch Hannah make order out of the chaos she's brought into my room, or I can head downstairs, find Jack, and shed some dignity for the sake of repairing our relationship. Neither one is all that appealing, but the truth is, I suppose it's about time I made up with my brother. I quickly excuse myself and prepare to be humbled.

# Chapter 10

I find Jack in the den with Brody, watching cartoons and messing with his hedgehog, Martha. Between his fingers, Jack's got a seriously fat mealworm, which he holds completely still until Martha tries to take it from him. That's when he sweeps his hand across her beady nose, sending her scurrying into the corner and Brody into fits of uncontrollable laughter. Then he freezes—until she comes waddling back, that is, and the game starts all over again.

"What are you guys doing?" I ask from the doorway.

"Feeding Martha," Brody says, still giggling. "Duh."

"How can you be feeding her if you don't let her eat anything?"

Jack's smile fades. He considerately tosses a mealworm over to where Martha's turned herself into a prickly little ball, then turns to me and says, "There? Feel better?"

I swallow hard, stung a bit by his tone. "Hey, Jack?"

"What?"

"Can I talk to you for a sec?" I shoot a look in Brody's direction. "*Alone?*"

"I'm busy," he says, digging through the plastic worm container.

"Just for a few minutes? Please?"

Jack throws another worm in Martha's direction. "Yeah, okay." He hands the container to Brody and says, "We still on for the Segathon later?"

Brody glares at me. "You know it."

I follow Jack into the kitchen. He rustles around the freezer, pulling out some vanilla ice cream, which he scoops into two tall glasses before topping them off with a fizzy helping of root beer. "So what's up?" he says, jamming a bendy straw into each glass.

My heart goes *thud-thud* in my chest. Jack places one of the ice cream sodas in front of me, which I guess is a good thing. Still, I feel like a kitten on caffeine, all jacked up on nervousness.

"Well?" he prods. His voice is cool and even, but not unkind. I take a deep breath.

"I'm sorry," I say. "I didn't mean to . . . insult her. Or you."

"She has a name, you know."

Is he trying to make this harder on me? "Yeah, I know. Hannah. Okay? I'm sorry I was so evil to her."

Jack's lips twist into a half smile. "I'm really not the one you should be apologizing to."

"But *you're* the one who hates me."

He shakes his head. "I don't *hate* you, Luce. I'm just . . . surprised, that's all."

"Daddy says I hated Echo, too," I point out. "At least, at first."

"Yeah?" Jack chuckles. "Yeah, I guess you did."

"So I cleared out some space for her—for Hannah—in my room. Our room. And I promise I'll be nicer. Just—don't be mad, Jack. I don't like it when you're mad at me."

Jack takes a long drag of frothy soda. "You gonna drink that?" he asks, gesturing to my untouched glass.

I feel my eyes dampen, and I know that if he doesn't say something nice to me in the next five seconds I'm going to cry. Thankfully, Jack speaks just before the first tear is about to fall: "So what do you say you and I do something tomorrow after you get out of school?"

"You and me?"

"Yeah, just the two of us. Sound good?"

The enormous weight of worry slides off my shoulders and down my back and crashes to the floor. I leap up and throw my arms around my still-seated brother's neck. "Sounds perfect!" I say, hugging him tightly.

"Yo, ease up there, Biscuit," Jack laughs. "You're gonna choke me!"

I let go and am just about to take my seat again when Hannah pokes her head into the kitchen.

"Um, am I interrupting anything?"

I suck on my soda, waiting for Jack to respond. He shakes his head. "Nothing major. Why?"

Hannah flashes me a semisheepish grin. "Well, I could use a little help moving some of my stuff downstairs."

And just like that, Jack's and my heartfelt conversation is over. He springs up and goes to Hannah, pausing briefly to turn and point his outstretched arm at me. "Tomorrow—you and me, right?"

"Right," I say, a lump forming in my throat.

I barely have time to feel sorry for myself before Mom wanders in to brew a cup of chamomile. "Hey, you," she says, dipping her trusty tea ball into the canister.

Just hearing her voice makes me want to crack open and let all the stuff gurgling inside me come flying out. I want to tell her about my impossible crush on Tobin Scacheri, and Tabitha's newly discarded virginity, and my cut-short reconciliation with Jack. I want to tell her about the zillions of different thoughts playing Twister in my head, and how they make me feel like I'm truly about to explode into millions of particles that will scatter like ice pebbles in a storm.

I want to say these things, but I don't.

Instead, I push my ice cream soda to the side and say, "Can you boil enough water for a second cup?"

Silently, my mother plucks the teapot off the stove,

pulls it under the faucet, and adds more water. When the kettle sounds its whistle, she pours water into her mug, dunks the tea ball a few times, then transfers it from her own mug to mine. "Honey or sugar?"

"Honey," I say. "*Lots* of honey."

Mom joins me at the table. She pulls the crossword puzzle from the paper and starts filling in the squares. I blow into my cup and watch her work.

"What's up, Luce?" she says after a few minutes. "You look like you need to say something."

"I was just thinking," I say, taking a tentative sip. "You've been drinking a lot of tea lately."

"Yes," she agrees. "I guess I have."

"So what is it? Is it *her*?"

"Who, Hannah?" Mom asks, putting her pen down. "Not particularly          re's just been a lot going on lately. Lots of c'

Mom gets                              the pantry, returning with a                                     She offers me some bu

"I j'                                          here," I say.

"                                       ne thinking." She p                              ks at the filling. "So,                                       e for Halloween?"

                              to go trick-or-treating."

                              o get dressed up for school?"

                              school now."

Mom smiles. "Oh, well, excuse me. I didn't realize we were too old to have fun anymore."

"I'll probably just stay here with you and Dad," I say. "That should be *loads* of fun."

"Ordinarily, I'd be thrilled," she says. "But Dad isn't going to be here—he and the boys have a two-week gig in the Poconos. They're leaving Friday."

"Friday? But they just got back."

"I know, honey. But it's his job."

I feel myself begin to pout. "I liked it better when he wasn't touring."

"Oh, you." Mom ruffles my hair. "If you didn't have something to complain about, you'd complain about not being able to complain."

"Where's Dad?" I ask. "You're being very mean."

"He's practicing at Bobbo's. And you're being very fourteen."

That's my cue to leave. "This family," I mutter, "is giving me an ulcer." I pretend not to hear my mother's laughter as I skulk out of the room.

# Chapter 11

"Ugh, what's that smell?" Allison says as we stroll into the cafeteria.

I take a deep whiff. "Taco Tuesday." We wrinkle our noses in unison.

One problem with going to the largest high school in the state is that the cafeteria is too small to accommodate all the students. So they split lunch into three periods. Allison and I were unfortunate enough to be assigned "A" lunch, which, ridiculously enough, actually begins at 11 A.M. Who wants to eat cafeteria tacos that early in the morning? Taco Tuesday is only a teensy bit better than Fried Rice Friday.

We get in line. At the beginning of the year, Allison and I brought our own lunches—something we quickly learned is a no-no at Haley. Only the dweeboids brown-bag it here, and dweeboids we are not.

It takes roughly half of our allotted twenty-five-minute lunch period to get two soggy tacos, a wad of wilted iceberg-lettuce "salad," and a mound of refried beans that look like moldy Alpo. We take our seats at the end of our regular table, which is situated between the junior jock-boy table and the sophomore band table. If the Kims had "A" lunch, they'd probably sit with the varsity cheerleaders—Kim Tate, of course, sacrificing her hockey squad to satisfy Kim Talbot's need to socialize with only the coolest of the cool. It's a group Ally and I would most likely never be offered entrance into, even though three short months ago, Kim Talbot was one of our best friends.

Ours is sort of the freshman free-for-all table, a bizarre mix of brainiacs, theater brats, student council reps—and us. A dozen identical avocado-colored trays are lined up side by side, their contents mostly untouched.

"This is disgusting," Allison says, pushing her tray away.

I nod empathetically. "Tell me about it."

"We should become vegetarians," she says. Vegetarians are the only brown-bagging group who escape torment.

"Yeah, but then we'd have to start eating tofu. And no more hamburgers. I don't know if I could give up hamburgers."

"Duh, Lucy," Allison says. "We wouldn't really *be* vegetarians. We would just pretend to be during lunch."

Our debate over the merits of going meatless is soon interrupted by Tabitha, who practically skips over to our table waving a small orange envelope.

"What are you doing here?" I say as she slips into the seat next to me. Ally's mouth forms a surprised O. I guess I forgot to tell her that Tabitha came over yesterday.

"I snuck out of class," Tabitha says panting. "I just couldn't wait to tell you."

"Tell me what?"

"Here." She hands me the envelope. On the front, in cramped, unfamiliar boy writing is a single, heart-fluttering word: "Biscuit."

I look up. "No," I say.

"Yes!" she says, grinning like an idiot.

"Are you going to open that?" Allison interjects. "I, for one, would like to get a clue as to what's going on."

I turn the envelope over and jimmy one corner open with my finger. *Breathe,* I remind myself, *breathe.* I see the corner of a card and slowly pull it out, savoring every second. "You are invited," it reads, silver glitter on a black background laced with cobwebs. My eyes drop to the next line: "WHAT: Tobin's 4th Annual Halloween Bash."

"Tabitha," I say slowly, "if this is a joke, I'm going to shave every single hair off your fuchsia head."

She laughs. "No joke, Luce," she says, holding up an identical envelope. "I got one, too."

"But how?"

"Andy Rockwell. Turns out Tobin used play on this

pickup basketball team with Andy's older brother, Adam. Anyway, Andy's in my photography class and he gave me these last period and told me to give one to you and so here I am and *oh my god*, what are you going to say to him?"

"Who?" Allison chimes in.

"Tobin Scacheri," Tabitha replies, still grinning.

"Tobin Scacheri!" Ally shrills.

"I don't have a costume," I say softly.

"We'll get you an effin' costume!" Tabitha says. "That's, like, so not important right now. Didn't you hear me? He's been *asking* about you. He *likes* you, dingus."

"I told her he liked her," Allison yells. "I told you, didn't I, Lucy?"

"Tobin Scacheri," I whisper, the words sliding over my tongue like half-melted Hershey's Kisses.

Allison shakes her head. "It's like I said, Lucy. The universe is taking care of you. The question is," she continues, tentatively munching her taco, "when is the universe going to start taking care of *me*?"

Tabitha and I exchange quick looks. "Well, of course you'll come with us," I say.

"Yeah, totally," Tab echoes. "You're with us."

Allison fingers the glitter on the invitation. "Nah," she says. "It would be too weird. I mean, I wasn't invited or anything."

Tabitha shrugs. "So we're inviting you."

"It's not the same," Ally says. "Besides, I'm baby-sitting that night."

"Can't you get out of it?" I ask.

She shakes her head. "It's okay, Lucy. Really. You'll go and you'll have an amazing time and then you'll call me and tell me all about it."

"I don't know," I say. "It won't feel right, you not being there."

There's an awkward silence while all three of us stare at the invite, placed on the table equidistant from each of us.

"Look," Tabitha says suddenly. "I should get back to class. Mr. Lefton will think I drowned in a toilet or something. But, Luce—we'll talk on the bus, okay?" She takes a few steps, then turns back and says, "Tobin Scacheri. Can you even believe this is your life?"

She runs off, and I sit there, dumbstruck, thinking, *No. No, I cannot.*

# Chapter 12

On the bus, Tabitha convinces me to get off at her stop so we can spend some time at her house making party preparations and planning my costume. "It has to be something you can look cute in, so no fake blood or anything," she advises. "But it should be creative, too, so you can't be a Gypsy or a kitten or anything."

Tabitha rifles through her closet and extracts a short velvety dress the color of crushed blueberries. "See this? This is going to be my costume." She reaches for a headband on the top of her dresser and puts it on. Two horns covered in red sequins sprout from her scalp. "Get it?" she asks, grinning. "I'm a devil with a blue dress on.'"

"Oh," I say. "Right."

Tabitha gives me an overexaggerated look of horror. "Come on, Lucy. You know the song." She sings a few bars, shimmying her hips.

"I know, I know. But I can't pull off something like that. It's not me."

Tabitha purses her lips a bit. "Yeah, I guess you're right." She puts the dress back and plops down

on her bed next to me. After a few minutes of point-
less brainstorming, she says, "Wings. You need to
have wings."

"What, like a fairy?"

"Not just any fairy," she says, totally juiced. "I don't
know why I didn't think of this before. I mean, it's
*so* perfect."

"What? What's so perfect?"

"Tinker Bell!" she squeals. "Wings and glitter and
sparkly tights that show off your legs. You have great
legs, you know."

"I do?"

"Definitely!" She puts an arm around me and gives
me a squeeze. "You'll see—Tobin Scacheri isn't going
to know what hit him."

"Mom!" I shout, dropping my book bag in the foyer.
"Mom, I need you!"

"I'm in here," she yells back from the kitchen. "And
stop yelling."

"There you are." I hug her as she stirs something
scrumptious-smelling in a wok. "Best mom in the
whole wide world."

"What do you want this time?" She tries to sound
stern but can't quite pull it off.

I fish a mushroom out of the wok and pop it into my mouth. "Costume."

"I thought you were too old for all that stuff."

"That was *before* I got invited to Tobin Scacheri's fourth annual Halloween bash."

Mom arches one eyebrow. "Tobin who?"

"Scacheri."

"And he is . . . ?"

"The person who's throwing the party." Mom switches eyebrows. "He's this guy I kind of know from school."

Mom looks into the wok, barely hiding her smile. "I see."

"So can you make me a Tinker Bell costume or not?"

"Ooh, good choice," says Hannah. I whirl around to see her quietly chopping tomatoes in the corner.

"You think?"

Hannah nods knowingly. "Totally."

I turn back to Mom. "Tabitha says I need a leotard. A green one. I'll also need—"

"Hey, where have you been, anyway?" Mom asks suddenly. "Your brother's been looking for you all afternoon."

A lead weight goes *thunk* in my stomach. I can't believe I forgot all about Jack's and my plans.

"I—I was at Tabitha's," I stammer. "Brainstorming costume ideas. Where's Jack? I should go apologize."

"He and Brody went to the arcade half an hour ago," she says. "You'll have to wait until dinner. After which we'll discuss this costume business."

Deflated, I retreat to my room, where I pretend to do my homework, and wait for my brothers to come home.

Jack and Brody breeze through the door literally thirty seconds before Mom sounds off, "Supper!" So I don't even get a chance to talk to him alone before everyone's crowded around the dining room table. I wait for Jack to say something—even a "What happened to you?" would be okay—but instead, he very pointedly ignores me and jokes with Grody about some pinball game they fed a zillion quarters into at the arcade.

"Jack," I say when there's a break in conversation. "Sorry about this afternoon. I got . . . unexpectedly busy."

"Whatever," he says, shrugging. "Gave me and the Brodster a chance to hang out." He grins at Brody, who beams in return. This makes me feel worse than

I already do—especially after my explosion the other day. I can't even enjoy my mother's fantastic ginger stir-fry.

Things get sort of tense and quiet for a minute. Then Dad clears his throat and says, "I got a call from Carlos today. Seems Angie's doctor told her she needs to stay off her feet for the next six weeks."

"Everything all right with the baby?" Mom asks, worried.

"Yeah. Just a precaution." He twirls some lo mein noodles around his fork. "Thing is, Carlos is convinced she's going to deliver sooner rather than later. He's pretty much glued to her side, so the combo's minus one for the time being."

"What about the gig? Do you have a backup?"

"Actually, I do." Dad smiles. "So how about it, Jack? Think you're up for a little road trip with your old man?"

Jack's eyes practically pop out of his head as he turns to Dad. "Are you serious?"

"Two weeks, twelve hundred dollars."

Now it's Brody's turn to gape. "Twelve hundred dollars!" he shouts.

"Quiet, Sparky," Jack play-growls. "I'm thinking here."

Dad's smile falters slightly. "What's to think about?

I figured you could use the money. What better way to get paid than to play?"

"Dad—my horn."

Dad waves him off. "Carlos says you can use one of his spares."

"What happened to yours?" I ask Jack. Of course, I'm completely ignored.

"So that just leaves . . ." Jack's voice trails off. He sneaks Hannah a shy look. "What do you think, babe?"

She chews on her bottom lip. It's like you can see the gears in her head slogging away. Finally she says softly, "Your dad's right—we could use the money."

Jack nods. "Are you going to be okay?"

She takes a swig of milk and nods. "I've got my hands full with half-made Halloween costumes. And someone's gotta take the little man out trick-or-treating."

Brody's eleven-year-old chest swells at Hannah's brown-nosing nickname. "Little man" my butt. Little beast is more like it.

"So," Jack says, grinning. "When do we leave?"

My fork hits my plate with a loud clank. "But you just got here!"

"You don't have to take it out on the dishes," Dad says lightly.

"I've lost my appetite," I say, looking down. "May I please be excused?"

"Don't go too far," Mom says. "You're on dish duty."

I skip the normal protesting and head straight for the sink. Mom follows not long after. We work side by side in a comfortably silent rhythm. Then, as I'm drying the wok, she says, "Hannah seems to think she can whip you up some wings."

"What?"

"To be honest, I'm not sure why she'd want to. You haven't been the most welcoming."

"But I want *you* to make my costume."

"Cut me a break, Lucy," she says, dumping the leftover stir-fry into a Gladware container. "You know how crazy things are around here when Dad's on the road."

I can tell by her tone that this is one battle I won't win. "Fine, Mother."

"You know, I can't for the life of me figure out why a girl with as pretty a face as yours would want to ruin it by pouting constantly."

"Flattery," I say, "will get you nowhere." I surrender my dish towel and retreat to what used to be my sanctuary of a bedroom, praying that Hannah's too busy sucking face with my brother to bother me tonight.

# Chapter 13

Thursday night around eleven, Hannah climbs the stairs and makes like she's getting ready for bed, just as she has done every night since she moved into my space. She comes into my room and changes into her pajamas—a pair of black soccer shorts and a hot-pink T-shirt with a glittery tiara ironed onto the front—and then heads for the bathroom, where she washes and rinses and splashes for fifteen minutes or so. When she returns, she pulls a book off the floor and reads until I turn the lights out. At this point, she says good night, to which I offer no reply save for a low grunt, and clicks on one of those battery-powered reading lights you can attach right to the book. After a sufficient amount of time passes, the light goes off. I hear Hannah quietly shut her book and tiptoe out, gently closing the door behind her.

Hannah returns sometime around 4:30 A.M., waking me up. I toss and turn for another hour or so, but the second I fall asleep my alarm goes off. I hit the snooze button over and over, groggy from sleep deprivation, and by the time I manage to drag my butt out of bed, Jack and my dad are already gone. If that's not bad enough, a quick look at the time tells me I'm in serious danger of missing the bus.

On the few days this has actually happened in the past, my mother has gone silently ballistic. She drives me to Haley with her lips pulled tight, dropping me off without so much as a wave. Worse, she refuses to write a note explaining why I'm late, so if I don't make homeroom roll call, I'm pretty much assured afternoon detention. For some reason, Mom fails to see the injustice of this.

"How many times do we have to have this discussion?" she'll ask, lips still tight even though they're moving. "School is your *job,* Lucy. It's your responsibility to be on time. And if you're not—well, then, you have to face the consequences."

So on top of not getting a goodbye hug from my dad, or a final (albeit brief) chance to make things up to Jack, who's pretty much been ignoring me since I accidentally blew him off, I end up—what do you know?—missing the bus. Mom is furious. "Dammit, Lucy," she says when I catch her in the bathroom. "I have an eight o'clock staff meeting, and I'm running late as it is."

Swears so rarely leave my mother's mouth that I know I'm in big big trouble. Which is why, when she tells me to wake Hannah and ask her if she can give me a lift, I do so with absolutely zero resistance.

Hannah, although bleary-eyed, seems agreeable enough. "Sure thing," she says, rolling out of bed. She fishes through a pile of rumpled clothes and extracts a pair of dark green sweatpants, which she pulls on right over her shorts, then slips a blood-red cardigan over her Pepto-pink tee. After stuffing her feet into a pair of beat-up black-and-white checkered Vans, she gurgles, midyawn, "Ready?"

"Are you sure you don't want to get changed?" I ask. "It's okay—I mean, we have enough time."

"Nah," she says, pulling her curls into a loose ponytail. "I'm just gonna come back here and crash anyway. *So* exhausted."

"I bet," I mutter.

Thankfully, Hannah grows slightly more alert once she's behind the wheel. But only slightly. "We have to get moving on your costume," she says, flipping through radio stations with one hand and adjusting her hair with the other. "Not much time left, huh?" I don't answer; my eyes are locked on her right knee, which, as far as I can tell, is the only thing steering the minivan at this very moment. She chatters on, but I'm so distracted by her lack of concentration that I'm not really listening. Her voice sounds like the "mwah-mwah" drone of all the adults on Charlie Brown specials.

We arrive at Haley in one piece; I wonder if my

mother's rekindled interest in her faith is responsible for that little miracle. "So," Hannah says, "sound good?"

"Uh . . . yeah," I say, not sure what I'm agreeing with. "Great."

Her face lights up. "Excellent. I'll see you later then, okay?"

"Yeah. Later."

Before I have time to dissect our bizarre exchange or even set foot in the lobby, I hear the braying ring of a bell. Through the glass, I see the last of the stragglers race to their respective homerooms. I step inside and with a feeling of dread begin the all-too-familiar sprint to E207.

The problem with sprinting to a second-floor homeroom with the threat of detention nipping at your heels is that it scatters your attention to the point where you can't see what's in front of you. And so, in the blur of the moment, it's very easy to miss the fact that you're about to collide with your crush object in the middle of a mold green stairwell.

Though he tries to dodge me, I barrel into Tobin Scacheri with a force that knocks him off his feet and takes me down with him. Tobin becomes a sort of human toboggan as we slide down the flight of stairs I had been taking two at a time. The world freezes in a moment of extreme pain, awkwardness, and humiliation.

But then he . . . laughs. *Laughs.* We're crumpled at the bottom of the steps, limbs tangled, our books and papers and other various supplies scattered in all directions, and Tobin Scacheri is letting out the most luscious laughter you could possibly imagine.

"We have to stop flying into each other like this," he says, rubbing the back of his head. *"Ouch."*

I cannot believe this is happening.

"Sorry," I say. "I'm so sorry." I can't even look at him. Instead, I stare at the frayed cuffs of his faded jeans.

"Don't worry about it," he says, rising. He offers me his hand, and once again, Tobin Scacheri is helping me up off the floor.

I slowly tear my eyes from the jean cuffs and let them land on Tobin's flushed face. He rewards me with a smile worthy of a toothpaste commercial, then hands me my backpack and some pens that managed to escape.

"Thanks," I say as I slip my arms into the straps. Tobin steps a little closer, or at least close enough for me to breathe in his scent—a curious mix of licorice and leather. My heart pitter-pats in my chest; my legs become liquid.

Tobin leans into me, his face slightly scrunched in concern. "You okay?" he asks, gently placing his left hand on my right elbow.

I blink a few times, unable to respond. "I think I'm late."

He nods. "Yeah. Me too."

Neither of us moves.

"You know what this means," he says.

"Detention?"

"You betcha."

It suddenly occurs to me that this, my third official conversation with Tobin Scacheri, also marks the third consecutive time that I've managed to make a complete and utter idiot out of myself in front of him. We stare at each other in silence.

"Well, okay," Tobin says finally, removing his hand from my elbow. "I guess I'll see you later. In detention."

"Right," I say, already missing his touch. "Detention."

Tobin's mouth curls into another smile, only this one doesn't reveal teeth. He winks one bottle-green eye, says, "Later, Biscuit," and takes off before I can steel myself enough to respond.

The day passes in excruciating slowness. Even lunch, which always flies by, seems to last for hours—due in part to Allison, whose rapid-fire questioning completely exhausts me.

"But how did he say it?" she demands. "Was it, 'See ya in detention!' Or was it more like, 'I'll see *you* in detention'?"

"Somewhere between the first and the second."

Allison sighs heavily. "But that could mean anything."

"Tell me about it." I push some limp broccoli stalks around my Styrofoam plate.

"Well, how did he *look* at you?"

"What do you mean?"

Allison rolls her eyes. "You know. Was it really intense? Or did he just look scared, like the next time you two met you might really cause some damage?"

"He's *not* afraid of me," I say.

"But how can you be sure? I mean, c'mon, Luce, even *I'm* beginning to think you're a little dangerous."

"Stop," I say. "It wasn't like that. He . . . winked at me."

"He *what?*" Allison practically shrieks. "He winked at you? Why didn't you tell me there was winking?"

"It's no big deal," I say, sending her into spastic fits.

"It is so a big deal," she protests. "When was the last time *you* winked at anybody?"

"I'm not a winker," I say. "So what?"

But it's all talk. Deep down, I know Allison's right. There was meaning in that wink. I can feel it in my elbow, still tingling from Tobin's touch. I can feel it in every part of my body, actually.

As Allison chatters on, I sneak a peek at the cafeteria clock. Eleven twenty-three. Three hours and fourteen minutes to go.

I can honestly say I've never looked so forward to Friday detention in my entire academic career.

# Chapter 14

After the final bell, I meet Tabitha by her locker and quickly fill her in on all the details.

"Oh," she says, tilting her head to one side. "Your first date—I'm so happy for you!"

"It's not a date," I say. "It's detention."

"Whatever." She fishes around in her purse, a small clutch constructed out of Astroturf-like material, and pulls out a slim gold wand of lipstick. "Here, put this on. And for god's sake, Lucy, will you lose the pony-tail? You're *fourteen* now."

Tabitha quickly extracts more items from her seemingly bottomless purse—a fold-up hairbrush, crystal butterfly earrings, a pocket-sized bottle of perfume—and goes to work right there in the hallway. Under ordinary circumstances, I'd feel too self-conscious for public primping. But then, these are no ordinary circumstances.

She swipes her thumb over the top of the lipstick and rubs the color onto my cheeks. "There," she says. "All done."

"I'm going to be okay," I say, more for my benefit than hers.

"Of course you are."

"Right."

Tabitha looks toward the row of buses, their closed doors indicating imminent departure. "Gotta run," she says, air-kissing my cheek. "But call me tonight and tell me *everything*."

I walk to detention slowly, deliberately. No more slipping on pencils or falling down stairwells for me, thanks. As I walk, my peripheral vision works over-time, desperately seeking even the slightest glimpse of Tobin Scacheri. No such luck. I reach my destination, suck in a great big breath, and enter the classroom.

Tobin Scacheri isn't in there.

In fact, *no one* is in there.

I pull the folded detention slip out of my back pocket. The room number is clear. N207. I step back-ward out of the room and check the black stencil above the door to make sure I'm in the right place. I am. So where's Tobin?

"Have a seat," bellows someone from behind me. I turn and see a gray-haired, stilt-walker-tall man with a Colonel Sanders mustache. He brushes past me and drops his bulging leather bag onto the teacher's desk with a dull thud. With crisp precision, he peels off his gray tweed jacket and folds it carefully over the back of his chair. His big eyes laser holes into me. "What are you waiting for, Miss Doyle? I asked you to have a seat."

I quickly slide into the desk closest to the door. How in the world did this gloomy gray giant know my name?

At exactly 2:57, the bell rings, sounding the official start of detention. I am still the only student in the room. The giant aims his laser eyes at me again.

"Welcome to detention, Miss Doyle. My name is Dr. Hooch, and I will be your warden for the next hour. My rules are simple: no talking, no gum chewing, and no homework. After all, this isn't study hall, it's detention. Any questions?"

Timidly, I raise my hand.

"Yes?"

"Am I it? For detention? I mean, in the whole school?"

Dr. Hooch unzips his bag sharply. " 'A' through 'F'."

"Excuse me?"

"I cover detention every Friday for students whose last names begin with letters 'A' through 'F'," he says, retrieving a newspaper. "I'm sure there are more of you serving time in other parts of the building."

Just my luck. Dr. Hooch buries himself in the arts and leisure section of the *Daily Journal,* and I dejectedly lay my head on folded arms. "Ah, ah, ah," Dr.

Hooch says from behind his paper. "Let me add to my previous rules—no sleeping, either."

I lift my head and, lacking better, Hooch-acceptable options, begin an inventory of the classroom. It's not nearly as fun as it sounds. After I've counted fifty-six visible linoleum floor tiles, my left eye detects motion in the door's tiny square window. I whirl around as two green eyes framed in Buddy Holly glasses appear.

Tobin.

When he sees me looking, he stands taller, so that his face fills the entire window. *Hey, you,* he mouths, chasing it with a heart-thumping smile.

*Hi.* I mouth back.

He beckons me with a curled finger. *Come here.*

*How?*

Tobin rolls his eyes playfully. *Bathroom.*

"Bathroom!" I blurt out. Dr. Hooch peers out at me over the paper. "I need to go to the bathroom. Very, very badly."

"Three minutes," he barks. "And counting."

Tobin Scacheri is waiting for me against the wall outside the door. "Walk," he whispers. I follow him down the hall.

When we're a safe distance from N207 he says, "I forgot you were a 'D'."

"What?"

" 'D.' For Doyle. Different detentions."

"Oh," I say. "Right."

"So it sucks, 'cause I was hoping I could be all slick and casually ask if you needed a ride home. Guess I blew that, huh?"

It takes a few beats for me to register what Tobin Scacheri is saying. His right shoulder leans against the wall; his hands are crammed into his pockets. He's a good six inches taller than me, but in this position, we are almost eye level with each other. And it's his eyes, those big green marble eyes, that are making it so difficult to comprehend what's actually taking place between us.

"So do you?" Tobin asks. "Need a ride?"

"Yes," I say. "I most definitely need a ride."

"Good," he says. "I'll meet you in the lobby, then. Okay?"

"Okay."

Tobin nods toward the classroom, and we begin to walk back. As we approach the door, he ducks out of view. "See you in a few," he whispers as I make my official return.

"Two minutes, fifty-six seconds," bellows Dr. Hooch. He taps his wrist. "Digital. One of the great inventions of modern times."

What a weirdo. I focus my attention on the window across the room, the one that overlooks the junior/senior parking lot. I pass the last half hour of detention trying to guess which of the remaining cars belongs to Tobin.

I guess I'll find out soon enough.

# Chapter 15

I am standing in the junior/senior parking lot watching Tobin Scacheri make a third attempt to unlock the passenger-side door of his 1972 Mercury Comet, which he proudly refers to as the Vomit. Huge saucers of rust have exploded from under the car's peeling white paint, and the rear right quarter panel is the color of a dull, purplish blue bruise.

"You own this?" I say to break the silence.

"Well," he says, shrugging. "She's not pretty, but she runs like a champ."

"I didn't mean . . . I like it. Her. My brother Jack would say she's got character."

Tobin looks up from the lock and grins. "You think? Yeah, that's kind of how I feel, too."

"Listen," I say. "Why don't I just get in on your side?"

He sucks in a chestful of air. "Yeah, okay."

I climb through Tobin's door and over the console, thankful I'm wearing jeans and not a skirt. The inside of the Vomit smells like burnt motor oil and coconut air freshener. Tobin turns the key in the ignition. The engine sputters for a minute, then gives out. He tries again. This time, there's an earsplitting pop, followed by a series of clicks and wheezes. Tobin's right foot pumps furiously, the engine engages, and we're off.

"Sorry about that," Tobin says.

"About what?"

"The car. She's not usually this temperamental."

"I don't mind."

Tobin grins again. "So how come you haven't rizvipped to my party yet?"

"Huh?"

"Rizvipped. RSVP'd?"

"Oh," I say. "I meant to."

"So are you coming?"

"Of course," I say. "I mean, yeah, definitely."

"Good. Great."

*Silence.*

Tobin fiddles with the dials on the radio. His fingers are long and slender, like my dad's. Sax-playing fingers. I try to focus on their shape instead of my nervousness, which is growing at an exponential rate. What should I say? "Gee, Tobin, that's an interesting tree, don't you think?" Ugh. It makes me realize that I hardly know this boy—even worse, that I'm completely devoid of any skills that would allow me to get to know him better.

I cannot wait to get out of this car.

We reach Capilano Street and I point out my

house. Tobin pulls up in front and puts the Vomit into park.

"Thanks for the ride," I say.

"No problem."

I try to open the door but it's still stuck.

"Here, let me try," Tobin says, reaching over me. His outstretched arm gently brushes my lap. His head is only a few inches from my own, so close that I can smell traces of shampoo on his hair.

I never *ever* want to get out of this car.

Finally, the door gives. I don't move. "Thanks again," I say. "I guess I'll see you later. At the party. Which I am coming to."

"Actually, I was thinking," Tobin says. "I only live a few minutes from here. Maybe I could give you a ride home after school sometimes."

A hot tingle strikes the insides of my stomach. "Really?"

"Yeah," he says. "Like tomorrow. I could give you a ride home tomorrow."

"Tomorrow's Saturday."

"Oh. Right."

"How about Monday?" I say quickly. "I could use a ride home Monday."

Tobin nods. "Monday's good. Meet me in the lobby again?"

"Sure," I say. "The lobby. Monday."

I slowly tear myself from the vinyl seat. Tobin reaches into the back for my book bag. Our hands meet briefly as I take it from him. "So, um, have a good weekend," I manage to mumble.

"Yeah, you too."

I think if he grins at me like that one more time, it will be totally acceptable for me to grab his face in my hands and mash my mouth against his. I really think that no one could possibly fault me for doing that.

He idles the engine as I walk away. I wonder if he's looking at me or if he's still fiddling with the radio. I'm too scared to sneak a peek, and like a total chicken I shut the door without so much as a glance back.

As Tobin roars off, I kick my sneakers onto the shoe pile in the corner, run into the den, and throw myself face first onto the couch. Did what I think just happened really happen? Did Tobin Scacheri, the beautiful blond boy with the Buddy Holly glasses, offer me door-to-door shuttle service on a semiregular basis? Even after I've caused him physical pain and killed any form of sustainable conversation? Why? Why would he do that?

There's only one rational explanation. My friends are right—he likes me. He may even like me as much as I like him.

Even the roots of my hair buzz with pleasure.

"There you are," Hannah says, materializing from nowhere and plopping down next to me on the couch, thereby terminating my crush buzz. "I thought maybe you'd forgotten."

"Forgotten what?"

She tugs on the tape measure draped around her neck. "Your Tinker Bell costume. Remember this morning? We made plans to work on it after school."

"Oh, right," I say. So *that's* what I'd agreed to.

"I've made some sketches," Hannah says. "Wanna take a look?"

I follow her into the kitchen. The table is buried under at least a dozen library books, a large drawing tablet, and a snowstorm of crumpled paper balls. Hannah flicks on the overhead light and pulls a pencil from behind her ear. "See," she says, waving me over, "I wasn't sure what kind of Tinker Bell you wanted to be."

"There's more than one?"

"God, yes. There's the Disney version, the Steven Spielberg version, and of course, the original." She lays out three detailed sketches, all of which have been delicately shaded with crayon. "So . . . what do you think?"

"Wow," I say. "These must have taken you all day."

"I know, I know. I went a little overboard."

"No—they're great. It's just . . . I don't get it."

Hannah tilts her head to one side. "Get what?"

"Why did you go to all this trouble? For me, I mean."

She smiles. "Believe it or not, this stuff's kind of fun for me. My mom's a designer for this theater school—she teaches classes there and does the costumes for all the shows. I learned to pin a hem before I could ride a bike. She always thought I'd end up doing the same thing—designing, I mean—but I got kind of burnt out on that artsy lifestyle. Hanging out with all the adults was fun when I was younger, but the older I got the more I realized that a lot of them are just oversized children."

Hannah's eyes are kind of glazed over, like she's all pulled up inside herself, and then suddenly she snaps to attention. "I need to take your measurements," she says. "Stand straight and raise your arms shoulder height."

I do as she says. Curiosity gets the best of me and I ask, "What did you mean about 'oversized children'?"

"Oh, that." Hannah shrugs, deftly pulling the tape measure around my waist. "Theater people—at least the ones I grew up with—have this certain . . . flavor. Everything about them is bigger and brighter and louder—their clothes, their hair, their speech. It gets very annoying, even when it's my own mother. Plus, everyone knows everyone else's business in Blue Lake.

Why do I need to keep track of who's in love with who else's boyfriend? It just gets old. And anyway, singing's a lot easier on my fingers than sewing."

"You sing?"

Hannah nods, whipping the tape measure around various limbs and making little notations on a piece of scrap paper. "That's why I enrolled at Berklee last year. I had this idea that I could be a modern-day Ella Fitzgerald or something." She chuckles. "That's how I met your brother, you know. He and the boys wanted a vocalist for a gig they got at Wally's."

"What's that?"

"It's this legendary jazz dive on Mass Ave—Jack didn't tell you any of this?"

"Nope."

Hannah's mouth twists slightly. "Weird." She looks back down at the sketches, pointing at the Disney Tinker Bell. "I'm thinking this is the one. Filmy white wings, lots of chiffon . . . you'll be such the glamour-puss."

I can't help giggling.

"So what do you say?" she asks, her eyes gleaming. "Think you can trust me?"

Though I'm not completely convinced, I shrug and say, "Why not?"

# Chapter 16

I'm a complete basket case for much of the weekend. All I can think about is Monday. Tobin and me, riding along in the Vomit. Me, desperately trying to keep my crazy nervousness in check.

What will I wear?

I spend most of Sunday trying to get ahold of my friends for some last-minute fashion advice. The phone rings just before dinner, and I pounce on it, hoping Tabitha will be on the line. But it's not her; it's Jack.

"Hi!" I say, a little too cheerfully. "How's the touring life?"

"Great," he says. "Really great, actually. Is Hannah around?"

His abruptness stings, but I can't give up that easily.

"Hey, Jack—remember that boy from homecoming? The one I tackled because I thought he was you? His name is Tobin Scacheri and he invited me to his Halloween party and gave me a ride home on Friday and I think you'd really like him." The words fall out of my mouth in a jumble, but I haven't talked to Jack at all since he left and I never did get a chance to explain about our botched afternoon of brother-sister bonding.

"That's great, Luce," he says flatly, like he's not really listening. "But can we discuss this later? I need to talk to Hannah and this call is costing a small fortune."

"Sure," I say through the huge lump that has formed in my throat. "Let me grab her."

To shrug off Jack's snub, I dive back into my closet and spend the next three hours perfecting a Tobin's-giving-me-a-ride-home-but-I-don't-want-to-look-like-I'm-trying-too-hard outfit. In the end, I decide on a long-sleeved black scoop-neck shirt and broken-in denim overalls. No jewelry, minimal makeup, and a pair of artfully messy braids dripping from either side of my head.

I can't even sleep, I'm so wound up. In my mind, I practice my conversational skills. There's the party— we could talk more about that. I think the PSATs are coming up, but honestly, is there anything *less* exciting than standardized tests? Tabitha suggested going the safe route—music, movies, and magazines—but what if the things I like are less cool than the things Tobin likes? What if he decides I'm too uncool to like? But when I voiced this fear to Allison, all she said was, "Well, Luce—I know I'm not as boy-savvy as Tabitha, but it seems to me that if you act like yourself and he thinks you're uncool, then why would you want to be with him anyway?"

This is what I'm thinking when I get to my locker Monday morning and see the note peeking out from between two grates on its door.

It reads: "Can't give you a ride today. Sorry. T."

Oh.

Two tiny tears form in the corners of my eyes, threatening to escape. I make tight fists with my hands, digging my fingernails into my palms. *I will not cry. I will not cry. I will not cry.*

But I am crying, just a little, when Tabitha arrives breathlessly outside her homeroom. Wordlessly, I hand her the note. She looks up at me, her face all sympathetic and soft, and says, "Maybe his mom asked him to run errands or something. You never know." She gives me a quick hug as the warning bell rings, before we retreat to our respective classrooms.

At lunch, Allison says, "You always assume the worst. Maybe he forgot he has to be somewhere else."

"But why didn't he just say that then?" I counter.

Allison pokes at the note, which is spread out on the table between us. "But see, he wrote 'today' — 'Can't give you a ride *today*.' Not 'Can't give you a ride' period. As in never. I'm sure you'll hear from him tomorrow."

Later, on the incredibly depressing bus ride home, I

lay this theory on Tabitha, who nods enthusiastically. "Plus he signed it 'T.' Initials are a good thing. It's sweet. You know?"

But I don't know, and what's worse is that I can't seem to shut off my brain. What did I do wrong? Was it something I said? Or did Tobin spring to his senses and decide he wants nothing to do with a flat-chested freshman whose older brother nicknamed her after a breakfast food?

I think these things as I lie in my bed Monday night, after halfheartedly completing my homework assignments and choking down a dinner for which I wasn't even hungry. The phone rings at eight, but it's only Jack, putting in his nightly call to Hannah. I stretch out flat on my back, with the lights off and the stereo spinning the Miles Davis CD he sent me for my birthday. *Kind of Blue*. It feels like the soundtrack to my life.

A little while later, Hannah knocks on my—strike that—*our* door and enters before I even ask who it is. "You feeling okay?"

"I've been better."

She flicks on the light and I squeeze my eyes shut to block it out. I feel the foot of my bed sag slightly as Hannah sits on it. "Do you want to talk about it?"

"No."

"Oh," she says. Then, after a couple of beats: "I finished your costume. Do you want to try it on?"

I sit up, blinking light into my eyes. "I don't know how to tell you this, so I'm just going to say it. I don't think I'm going to the party." My body tenses; I'm expecting Hannah to freak. Instead, she says softly, "Lucy, what *happened?*"

Silently, I reach into the top drawer of my nightstand, pull out Tobin's note, and hand it to her. She reads it over, then says, "I don't get it." I fill her in on the details.

"Oh, honey," she says, giving me one of those smiles that are supposed to comfort you but end up making you feel even more pathetic. "I'm not sure how you zipped from 'I can't give you a ride' straight over to 'I think you've got cooties.' "

I scowl. "I didn't say 'cooties.' "

"Yes, but you're convinced that this has something to do with his feelings for you, when it's ninety-five percent likely it has nothing to do with you at all." Hannah refolds the note and drops it back into the drawer. "You know, you could just call the guy. Ask him what's up."

"I am *not* calling Tobin Scacheri."

"Why not?"

"Because . . . because then he'd know. That I like him."

"And that would be bad *why?*"

"Because what if he doesn't like me?"

Hannah laughs, then quickly stifles herself. "I'm sorry. I'm not trying to make fun of you. Believe me, I know it sucks when you can't figure out what a boy is really thinking. But if you want my advice, don't abandon hope just yet. Not until you're perfectly certain there's no other reasonable explanation." She yawns and rises. "I hear a hot bath beckoning. Lights on or off?"

"Off," I tell her. "I think better in the dark."

She sighs. "You are so much like your brother, you know. Same quirks and everything. Same stubbornness, too."

"Get used to it," I say. "That's not a Jack thing. That's a Doyle thing."

Hannah nods, pressing a hand to her stomach. "Yeah, I'm beginning to figure that out."

There's a sharpness to her tone that catches me a bit off guard. Hannah takes a long, deep breath and says, "I think I'm going to take that bath before I get any grouchier."

When the lights go out, I turn over onto my stomach, squish a pillow between my arms, and promptly fall into a restless sleep.

Even though I obsessively check my locker at least half a dozen times Tuesday morning, there's not a

111

single supplemental Tobin note to be found. If that's not bad enough, Tabitha grabs me between classes and says, "Well, he's here. I don't know if that means anything, but I thought you'd like to know."

I mope my way through the rest of the day, and when I trudge onto the ancient yellow school bus, I'm so completely depressed that even Tabitha's a little wigged. "Dag, Lucy," she says. "I've never seen you so moony in your whole *life*."

Right before the bus pulls away, something loud rattles against our window. "Holy smack!" Tabitha shouts. "That's Tobin!" I crane my neck and see the aforementioned Tobin Scacheri pitching pebbles from the sidewalk and waving—I presume—to get my attention. My stomach lurches into my throat. I am in complete and utter shock.

"What are you waiting for?" Tabitha squeals, pushing me out of our seat and into the aisle. "Get out there!"

I hobble off the bus literally seconds before it lurches toward the exit.

"Hey," I say.

"Hey," Tobin says.

And that's it.

We stand there, not talking, me focusing on his shoes and him focusing on—well, I don't even know what, because I'm too busy studying the intricacies of his navy blue Pumas.

"Let me get your books," he says finally, reaching for my bag, which is so heavy it makes one of my shoulders dip lower than the other.

"Uh, okay."

Tobin starts walking toward the junior/senior parking lot, and I follow him in a half daze. He opens the back door, tosses both our backpacks in, then opens the passenger door for me. "You fixed it," I say.

"Yeah. Over the weekend. I figured it would make things easier."

He grins at me, and my legs get all wobbly, looking at him looking at me through his chunky black glasses.

"Thanks," I croak, sliding into my seat.

My seat.

"I'm glad I caught you," Tobin says as he buckles himself into the driver's side.

"Yeah?"

"Sorry about yesterday. I totally forgot I had this dentist appointment right after school. Have you ever had your gums scraped? Everything in my mouth still hurts. All I could eat at lunch was green Jell-O and some of those crusty reconstituted mashed potatoes."

I must be sporting the world's largest smile, because

Tobin sneaks a look at me and says, "Is there something inherently funny about reconstituted mashed potatoes?"

"Oh. No. No. I . . . I . . . know what you mean. About the gum-scraping stuff? I mean, the pain. The Jell-O. *Ouch*."

If it wouldn't attract too much attention, I think I'd smack my head against the dashboard. Could I *be* any more bumbling? I mean, really. *Pull it together, Doyle. Pull it together* now.

"So," Tobin says, taking the right onto Basin Road. "Do you have to go home right away? Or could we, you know, go somewhere else first?"

"Sure," I say. "Wherever."

So instead of heading right on Route 273, Tobin makes a left and drives straight through the heart of Old New Castle. I'm fairly certain that he's taking me to Battery Park. And boys don't take girls to Battery Park unless they (A) are family or (B) want to make out.

Score!

Tobin eases the Vomit into a parking spot that's smack in the middle of the loop. "Let's walk."

We stroll down a path that zigzags through the park. I've walked this path a zillion times, but my feet are so unsure of themselves that this feels like the first. There's a weird silence between us, and I keep waiting for Tobin to break it, but he doesn't. Finally I say, "I hear the PSATs are coming up."

Tobin shoots me a strange look—and rightly so. I can't be certain, but I'd guess that I'm redder than his cherry-colored T-shirt. I feel like a total idiot.

"Yeah," he says. "I guess they are."

More silence.

"You like basketball," I say, trying again. "Right?"

"Yeah. Who told you that?"

*Busted.*

"Um, my friend Tabitha told me that you used to play with Andy Rockwell's brother Adam." I say this sentence so fast that the words kind of bleed into each other.

"Right," he says. "Yeah, me and Ad Rock go way back."

I immediately pick up on the Ad Rock reference, as Jack is obsessed with a musician who goes by the same nickname. So I brave a question that has some actual merit: "Do you listen to the Beastie Boys?"

"Hells yeah," he says. "*Paul's Boutique* is definitely one of my Top Ten Desert Island Discs."

Finally! A tiny speck of common ground.

"Really? I mean, it's a great CD and all, but sometimes I think I prefer *Ill Communication*." I blather on for at least a minute, talking about how the group got involved in the Free Tibet movement, and how it "energized their sound." I'm grasping at straws, basically parroting things I've heard Jack talk about over the years. But I'm not being totally dishonest—I really do love both of those albums. It's just that while Jack's into deconstructing somebody's sound, I'm content to simply listen to it.

Tobin nods. "You know, I never thought about it like that, but you're totally right. I don't know. I don't get that deep about music. Mostly I just listen to what I like, you know?"

Oh, the irony. But at least we're finally *talking*.

Tobin's comment gives me the perfect segue into my family's musical roots, so I tell him about Dad and the jazz combo, and how Jack's following in his footsteps. Which leads Tobin to tell me all about his mom, who's an art conservator at Winterthur but who's been working on a special assignment at the Brandywine River Museum. When I mention that I've never been there, Tobin says, "We should go sometime. Mom's working on a couple of the paintings from the Wyeth collection. The one she's doing right now is called *Roasted Chestnuts*, and it's just this guy staring out into the distance, roasting his nuts." I can't help it; I actually giggle. Tobin smiles and nudges me lightly with his shoulder. "You know what I mean. Anyway, it's very beautiful, this painting. All somber. I don't know, something about it just gets under my skin. You know?"

"Actually, I think I do. There's this CD Jack gave me for my birthday. It's by Miles Davis and—"

"Wait!" Tobin interjects. "It's *Kind of Blue*, right?"

"Yeah, how'd you know?"

"It's only the quintessential Miles Davis. And yeah, when I listen to it, it makes me feel exactly how I do when I look at that painting."

We're standing under a huge, sprawling willow tree when he says this, one that still has some green bits on its mostly naked branches. I'm thinking that if Tobin were to kiss me today, now would be the most perfect moment to do it. I'm actually sending psychic signals in his direction. *Kiss me, kiss me, kiss me.*

Instead, he looks at his watch. "Whoa!" he says. "It's almost five-thirty."

"No way," I say. "We've been here that long?"

"It *is* getting kind of dark."

We head back to the Vomit without Tobin so much as trying to hold my hand. Any connection I felt to him five minutes ago has completely dissipated. I'm back to feeling like a completely unhip doofus who has, in Tobin's eyes, zero girlfriend potential and a total lack of kissability.

But then, as he drives me home, Tobin starts telling

me about how his mom not only saves other people's art, but how she paints these amazing eighteen-foot-tall canvases of her own. "She's shown a few of her collections locally," he says proudly. "She even sold a piece to one of the du Ponts."

"Wow," I say, duly impressed.

"Sometimes we paint together on the weekends. For me it's just messing around, but I don't know. I kind of like it." He shoots me a sideways glance. "You know, I've never told anybody that I do that."

"Really? Why not?"

"Because it makes me sound like such a mama's boy or something."

"That's silly," I say. "I mean, my mom's a photojournalist, but it's not like we ever go out and take pictures together. I think it's really cool that you and your mom can bond like that."

"Yeah?" he says, like he's pleased that I approve.

"Yeah."

"You know, you're easy to talk to," Tobin says.

"I am?"

"Yeah," he says. "You give off this vibe, like you're completely . . . *real*. No fake girl stuff. I felt it the first time we ran into each other."

"Literally," I say, grinning.

"See?" he says. "You can laugh about that. Most of the girls I know aren't that cool."

I momentarily lose the ability to breathe. This also means I lose the ability to converse intelligently. It's okay, though, because for the first time, silence feels good instead of uncomfortable. It's like an I'm-too-busy-smiling-to-talk kind of silence.

We pull into my driveway, and Tobin walks me to the door. I look at him, steeling myself for a kiss I now feel is inevitable. But instead of laying one on me, Tobin says, "I promised I'd help out at my cousin Tiny's garage after school the rest of the week, so I can't drive you home. But I'll see you Saturday, right?"

"Right," I say.

Tobin rocks back and forth on his feet. "Yeah, so I'll see you then."

"Yeah, see you."

And then he leaves. He *actually* leaves.

*Without a single kiss.*

Talk about mixed signals.

"You're overreacting," Tabitha says when I call and whine to her about Tobin's failure to go in for the lip lock. "For god's sake, all the guy could eat today was Jell-O. Maybe his mouth was too sore to go mashing into yours."

This is true. Tabitha's other line rings; it's Elliot. "I

want to talk to the boy before my mom gets home," she says. "But promise me you'll stop obsessing so much, okay?"

"I promise," I say, fingers firmly crossed.

Because really—who in their right mind *wouldn't* be obsessing about Tobin Scacheri right now? Who pretty much asked me on a *date* to his mother's museum. Who not only secretly likes to paint, but who trusted me enough to confide in me about his hobby.

Who should've kissed me under that willow tree. Or at the front door. So why didn't he?

"I don't know, Luce," Hannah says later as she's sticking pins into my Tinker Bell costume, completing the final alterations. "Maybe Tobin's just a gentleman like that. Not all boys kiss on the first date, you know. Hell, it took Jack almost three weeks before he got up the guts to kiss me."

"Jack's always been big on that old-fashioned romantic stuff," I tell her. "He used to give me mini-lessons, like 'A boy should always open the door for you' and 'Don't put up with some punk who doesn't call when he says he will.' "

"Oh, the irony," she mutters.

"What?"

"It's nothing," she says, in a faux-breezy tone. "Just that Jack was supposed to call four and a half hours ago."

"What's that work out to in seconds?" I tease.

Hannah smiles. "Point taken. I guess I just miss him."

"At least you get to talk to him. I tried to tell him about Tobin the other night and he totally blew me off."

"Sounds like Jack all right."

I bite my bottom lip. Lately, the mere mention of Jack's name seems to make Hannah crabby.

"That should do it," she says, rising. "Be careful not to stick yourself when you wriggle out of that thing."

"Okay," I say. "Oh, and Hannah?"

"Yeah?"

"He'll call. They probably picked up a last-minute gig or something. Mom will tell you. When the combo's on tour, their schedule is always crazy."

"Sure," she says. "You're probably right."

At least, I hope I am.

# Chapter 17

The rest of the week rolls by with excruciating slowness, but somehow I make it to Saturday. The day of Tobin Scacheri's fourth annual Halloween bash. Or T-Day, as I've begun to think of it.

I shoot out of bed around nine-thirty, only forty-five minutes after my alarm first goes off. Not bad. Normally, I hate waking up to an alarm on weekends (I've been known to delay consciousness until as late as three in the afternoon), but I'm not sure how much party prep time I'll need.

I wander down to the kitchen and pour myself a bowl of Count Chocula. The house is silent. According to the note my mother has stuck on the fridge, she's off shooting the Halloween parade in Newark, Hannah decided to tag along, and Brody's Sega-ing in the basement and could I please keep an eye on him? Not the most difficult feat since the little booger eater tends to go catatonic in front of the set for hours and hours of game time.

As I slurp up the chocolaty milk at the bottom of my cereal bowl, I riffle through Mom's shoe box of recipes. She's insisted I bring something to Tobin's party—she's so old-school—and I figure Gram's triple-fudge brownies are more appealing than a three-liter bottle of generic ginger ale.

After procuring the recipe and gathering all necessary ingredients, I roll up the sleeves of my flannel pj's and get to work. First, I sift together the flour, baking powder, salt, and dry milk not once, not twice, but three times. Then I break chunks of unsweetened, semisweet, and milk chocolate into the top half of Mom's battered double boiler. I turn the knob on the range, checking the flame to make sure it's not too high. Finally, I fill the bottom portion of the boiler with water and set the contraption on the stove. The chocolate begins to melt, and I stir the gooey lump with a wooden spoon. I feel positively domestic.

The phone rings; I stretch my left hand to get it, still stirring with my right.

"Hey, it's me," Tabitha says. "Whatcha doin'?"

"Baking brownies," I say. "For the party."

Tabitha snorts. "Well, aren't we the good little Girl Scout?"

"It wasn't my idea—it was my mom's."

"Yeah, right," she says. "You should've gone with pumpkin pie—my sister says it makes guys horny."

"Tabitha! I'm not interesting in making anybody horny."

"Check your nose, Pinocchio," she says, laughing. "Is it growing yet?"

"Whatever. Look, can I call you back? I'm kind of at a crucial stage."

"Yeah, okay." *Click.*

When everything's been sufficiently sifted, stirred, melted, and beaten, I carefully fold the various components into a big orange mixing bowl. I say carefully because Gram's recipe specifically states that you can only turn the batter fifteen times—any more and the brownies won't rise properly. Then you must let the whole concoction rest for exactly thirteen minutes before gently transferring it into two square pans that have been greased and lightly dusted with a mixture of flour, cocoa, and powdered sugar.

I set the timer, then start working on the growing dish pile in the sink. The soothing sound of running water is soon interrupted by the mad stomp of size-seven feet as they bound up the basement stairs.

"What are you cooking?" Grody Brody asks, blowing a gigantic purple Bubble Yum bubble.

"I'm busy," I tell him.

He sucks the bubble in through his teeth, setting off a series of loud pops. "What are you cooking?" he repeats.

"None of your business."

A third time: "What are you cooking?"

I feign deafness, but he persists, chanting, "What are you cooking?" over and over again until I reach my breaking point. *"Will you please get out of my kitchen?"*

Brody blinks a few times, cracks his gum, and says, "Um, no."

I take a deep breath and change tactics. "Look, twerp. Mom left me in charge, okay? So don't push me."

"Oh yeah?" he scoffs. "What are you gonna do? *Batter* me to death?" He starts cracking up over his own lame pun.

"I'm warning you."

*"I'm warning you,"* he mimics in falsetto.

"When are you going to grow up?"

"When are you gonna grow boobs?"

That does it. I hurl the soapy scrub pad at him. It hits him smack in the eye. Any normal eleven-year-old would say "Ow" or throw something back at me. But not Brody. He brings his hand up to the target eye and brushes away some lingering suds. Then he takes a few steps toward me, sticks his index finger deep within his right nostril, takes it back out, and plunges the booger-infected hand into my meticulously prepared triple-fudge brownie batter.

The timer dings.

"You are *so* dead!" I scream. He shrieks and races

toward the basement door, knocking the bowl of batter to the floor. I slip on the chocolaty slickness as I charge toward the beast but still manage to grab the tail of his T-shirt at the same time his hand touches the knob. I yank him toward me, causing his knees to buckle. Brody wriggles around so that he's facing me, and as he tries to defend himself, his unclipped fingernails end up scratching my face. Then, as he scrambles to his feet, his head butts my lip. He starts pounding on me, and when I try to push him off, my palm thrusts upward, accidentally smashing his nose and sending him reeling.

There is blood *everywhere*.

"Ohmigod, ohmigod, ohmigod," I say, scrambling toward him. "Are you okay? Is it broken? Are you okay?"

*"What did you do to him?"*

Mom's home.

"Lucy Alexis—what did you do? *What did you do?*" Mom dashes to his side and I promptly explode in a flurry of tears.

"He boogered my brownies," I say, sobbing.

She ignores me. "Hannah, get me a towel. And an ice pack—they're in the freezer."

Hannah brushes by me to retrieve the items. "I didn't mean to hurt him," I say.

Mom takes the ice pack from Hannah, wraps it in

the kitchen towel, and applies it to Brody's bloodied nose.

"It was an accident," I say, sniffling.

"I don't want to hear it, Lucy," Mom barks.

"But—"

"*Enough,*" she says. "I want you to clean up this mess. *Now.*"

I head to the cleaning-supplies closet for a giant sponge as Mom and Hannah usher Brody to the upstairs bathroom to finish doctoring him. In a few minutes, Hannah reappears in the kitchen. "It's not broken," she says. "But that must've been a hell of a shot."

"It really was an accident," I say, sponging up the last of my ruined batter. "You don't think she'll tell me I can't go to Tobin's party, do you?" I look to Hannah for confirmation, but her mouth just drops wide open.

"Lucy—your face!"

My fingers fly up to my cheek. As they do, they brush a particularly large lump on my bottom lip. I grab the shiny stockpot that always rests on our stove because it's too big to fit into any of the cabinets and look at my reflection. The kid got me good. His nails have left three angry red welts across my skin, like war paint. My throbbing lip lump is yellowish purple. I am hideous.

Fresh tears pour from my already reddened eyes.

Hannah slips behind me to give me a comfort hug. Then, midhug, she abruptly pulls back. "Um, Lucy? Don't freak, but, . . . there's a wad of gum in your hair."

"*What?*"

"Hold still a second—maybe I can get it out." Her fingers gently tug at a clump of hair a few inches above my neck. *Ouch.*

"It's in there pretty deep," she says. "I think we'll have to ice it."

I nod and go to chew on my bottom lip—an old nervous habit—sending shooting stabs of pain to the lump. A zillion thoughts are turning around my mind: How long does it take to ice out gum? What if it doesn't come out? Will ice erase the welts on my cheeks, too? What in the world can I do about my new friend, the lip lump?

And of course, the biggest question of all: How can I go to Tobin Scacheri's Halloween party as a battered Tinker Bell?

Mom returns to the kitchen, looking worn out but infinitely less angry.

"Well," she sighs, leaning against the entryway. "Let's just hope the neighbors don't call Child Protection Services."

"How's Brody?"

"He's fine. He's getting changed to go over to Stu's house."

"I'm really sorry, Mom," I say in a hoarse whisper. "I didn't . . . I didn't mean to hurt him like that. Honest."

"I know you didn't mean to," she says. "But Lucy—you're bigger and you're older and I left you in charge."

"There's more," I say. "Gum. In the back of my head." I turn around to show her the hairy purple glob.

"Oh, honey," Mom says with another sigh.

Hannah pipes up, "I thought we could ice it out."

"If it was Trident, maybe, but this wad is *huge*." A third sigh. "I guess it can't hurt."

As Mom prepares the ice, Hannah runs upstairs to get some vitamin E oil. "It'll keep those scratches from scarring," she tells me as she smears the sticky goop across my cheeks.

"Gross," I say.

My mother hands me a pair of rubber gloves and tells me to put them on, then slips two oven mitts over my hands. Next, she hands me some ice cubes nestled in a thick stack of paper towels and directs my hand to the gum wad. "Have a seat," she says. "This'll probably take a while."

Thirty minutes and four ice cube treatments later, we finally admit defeat.

"Phase two," Hannah decrees. "Peanut butter."

When the PB fails, Mom suggests mayonnaise. When that doesn't work, Hannah asks her if we have any lighter fluid in the house. "I think I read somewhere that it de-stickifies resins and whatnot."

"I've read that, too," Mom agrees. "Check the upstairs linen closet."

"Hold on a second," I say, finally shedding some patience. "Is that even safe?"

"As long as no one lights a match, you should be fine."

I take a peek at the sunflower clock hanging above the sink. It's nearly one-thirty—only five and a half hours until T-time. I close my eyes and try not to cry as the nauseating smell of peanut butter and mayo doused in lighter fluid hits my nose.

# Chapter 18

It's going on two when Mom gives Hannah a twenty and the keys to the van. "There's a Hair Cuttery down Route Thirteen," she says. "Tell them to be gentle, please."

"Well, what do we have here?" says Varma, my aging bleached-blond hair surgeon. "Sugar, this mess is *deep*."

"What do you think?" Hannah asks. "Can we keep any of the length?"

I watch Varma's screwed-up face in the mirror as she surveys my head. "Maybe," she says. "Lots of shaggy layers might do the trick."

One of Hannah's delicate eyebrows shoots up. "Shaggy?"

"It's either that or it all comes off. Your call."

"Just do it," I say. "Cut it all off."

"That's pretty short, Luce," Hannah says. "It won't even hit your earlobes."

"Could be cute," Varma muses. "Like one of them pixies."

Hannah nods. "Like an undercut, with the bottom

layer cropped close." She snaps her fingers. "Ooh—
and bangs would be adorable."

But I don't feel adorable, not when Varma rubs
some kind of peppermint shampoo into the hair salad
already fermenting on my head, and not when I
see the first long locks fall to the linoleum under
my chair. To keep from crying, I close my eyes and
listen to the R & B playing on the Hair Cuttery's
speaker system. My remaining strength drains with
each snip, and I picture Tobin Scacheri's beautiful
face contorting as he laughs meanly at my newly
shorn hair.

"Tuck your chin in, sugar," Varma says. "I gotta
chop the front now."

*This is it*, I think, *the final sign*. The last in a long series of omens telling me that I shouldn't be wearing
some stupid leg-baring getup to Tobin Scacheri's stupid Halloween bash.

"Hannah?" I say, eyes still closed.

"A little shorter on the sides," she says—to Varma,
I presume. "So they'll have a gentle curve to them."

"Gotcha."

"Hannah?"

"Little more," she says.

I try again. "I don't think—"

Hannah railroads over my words. "Let's see it dry."

Within seconds, Varma's rolling what's left of my

hair around a hairbrush and applying loud heat. The back of my exposed neck burns under the hot air. I can't bear to look.

Finally, Varma clicks the hair dryer off. "Not bad," she says.

"Take a look, Luce," Hannah says.

Tentatively, I open one eye and see nothing but chin. I blink a few times, take in the whole picture and nearly faint. It's gone. All of it. Maybe six inches of caramel strands hang smoothly on the sides of my head. Not enough to mask the angry Brody welts across my cheek.

"Perfect," Hannah says, fluffing the sides a bit. "Don't you think?"

I don't answer. I don't know what to say. I've always, *always* had long hair. I feel . . . *naked* without it.

"What time is it?" I ask when we get back into the car.

"Little after three."

I pull down the passenger-side visor and flip open the cosmetic mirror to examine my new do again. It's not completely heinous. I swivel, check my hair out from different angles, and tuck the sides behind my ears. The bangs are so short. I wonder how long it will take for them to grow back.

"We could play with the color," Hannah says. "Add some light blond streaks in the front. When I was in high school, I used to paint my friend Natalie's hair all the time."

"Okay."

"Yeah?" She grins. "We could even do it today—we have plenty of time."

"Can Tabitha help? She's really good with that kind of thing."

"Absolutely!" Hannah beams at me. "We'll call her as soon as we hit the house."

Only there's no need, because Tabitha bombards us the minute we enter our front door.

"Where have you two been?" she shouts. "We only have *four* hours and—Ohmigod, look at you!"

I feel every ounce of blood in my body rush to my face. "You hate it."

"Are you kidding?" Tabitha squeals. "You look awesome."

Mom wanders in from the den, a book of crossword puzzles tucked under her arm. "So let's see it." I walk over to her. Mom's face is completely blank. She fingers the supershort bangs framing my forehead. "Didn't I say 'Be gentle'?"

Hannah steps in. "I know it's a little extreme, but it was either this or some multilayered Farrah Fawcett throwback."

Mom shakes her head, still staring at my hair. "This

should teach you not to horse around with Brody again anytime soon."

But there's no time to worry about that now. Hannah, Tabitha, and I head upstairs and lock ourselves in the bathroom. Hannah takes the drugstore hair-painting kit we just bought and puts some smelly purple goop in an old mixing bowl from the kitchen. "Shouldn't that stuff be yellow?" I ask.

Tabitha rolls her eyes. "They make it purple to tone down the brassiness. You know, complimentary opposites? On the color wheel."

"Oh."

Hannah ditches the kit's wide-bristled brush and opts for a thin one she extracts from a makeup bag. I sit on the toilet as she and Tab debate the usefulness of tinfoil. "It keeps the color from bleeding," Tabitha argues.

Hannah frowns. "Yeah, but the box says not to get the stuff near 'reactive metal.' Is foil reactive?"

"Trust me," my fuchsia-haired friend says. "I do this, like, *all the time*."

In the end, Tabitha grabs a roll of Reynolds from the kitchen and uses a pair of orange-handled scissors to cut the stuff into small squares. She and Hannah form a sort of mock assembly line: separate, foil, paint, fold, repeat. It takes nearly forty minutes before the front of my head flops with silver.

"What now?" I ask.

Hannah checks her wristwatch. "Now we wait."

Another twenty minutes pass before they begin unwrapping me. In the interim, I give Tabitha my account of the showdown with Brody. "What a dork," Tab says, disgusted.

When the foil has been discarded, she and Hannah vacate so I can shower out the crusty dye. I'm surprised at how weightless my head feels as I work in a big glob of vanilla shampoo. Maybe this cut is a good thing after all. Maybe Brody's bubble gum was just a blessing in disguise.

I turn off the water, step out of the shower, and begin to towel off. Steam clouds the mirror. I wipe a small circle clean to check on Hannah's artistry and nearly pass out.

*Orange.*

How could this have happened? I know for a fact that purple and orange aren't anywhere near each other on the color wheel.

Tabitha knocks on the door. "Luce? Are you almost done in there? I really have to pee and Brody's hogging—"

I swing the door wide; Tabitha gasps loudly. I am in a total panic. "What am I going to do?" Tabitha herds me back into my room. Hannah is sprawled on her bed, flipping through a magazine. She looks up, spots the tangerine clumps striping my hair, and groans. I stand there, wrapped in a terry-cloth towel, shaking violently, trying not to start crying yet again. She rises and pokes through the wet strands to check out the damage. "I knew we shouldn't have used foil," she mutters.

"It wasn't the foil," Tabitha says crossly. Then she gasps. "The mixing bowl—it was metal! That must have caused the reaction!"

"Who cares what did it?" I wail. "It's like I'm cursed! Like I'm not meant to go to this party."

"What?" Tabitha places her hands firmly on her hips. "You cannot be serious, Lucy. I mean, you're *not* chickening out now. I won't let you."

I wish Allison were here instead of baby-sitting her bratty cousins. Allison would tell me I was right, let me cry on her shoulder, blow up a bag of microwave popcorn, and slide *Grease* into the DVD player. Allison would not be turning my bedroom into a beauty boot camp. She would not be slicking glittery gold hair gel over my orange-striped hair, or sponging shimmery foundation on my face, or painting black liquid liner on the top lids of my eyes. And she most certainly would *not* force me to examine my reflection, especially in the state I'm in.

Hannah shakes her head in amazement. "Good god, child. I don't know how we did it, but you look fabulous."

I take a deep breath before inspecting the final results. It's a miracle, but they actually pulled it off. Between Tabitha's glitter gel and Hannah's artful
makeup application, my hair looks like it's *supposed* to
have a brassy glow. They've also managed to erase all
traces of Brody's battering. In fact, I think I may actually look—dare I say it?—*good*.

"Thank you," I say, giving them both the world's
biggest hugs.

"Careful there," Tabitha says. "You mess up that
face and you're on your own."

It's nearing seven. Hannah turns her attention to
Tabitha as I pull on my costume: sparkly green tights,
a dark green sequined bodysuit, and an itty-bitty skirt
constructed of dozens and dozens of sheer fabric trian-
gles, hand-dyed by Hannah in at least six shades of
green. Tab tosses me a tube of silver body glitter,
which I daub on patches of bare skin as she steps into
her skintight velvet minidress. Hannah flits between
the two of us, securing Tabitha's cherry red wig with
bobby pins, fastening the Velcro straps of the great big
wings she made me that look as if they're actually
sprouting from my back. When she's finished, her face
is covered with a thin film of sweat. We've completely
worn her out.

I slip on my dyed-green slippers at exactly 7:03.

"C'mon," I say, tugging on Tabitha's arm. "We're gonna be late!"

"Don't be silly—we can't leave here for at least another thirty minutes."

"What? Why not?"

Tabitha gives me a *you-are-so-clueless* look. "Lucy, we're *freshmen*. Going to a *junior's* party. If we show up on time, we'll just look pathetic."

And so the three of us troop down to the kitchen. Somehow my wise mother thought to order us a pizza, which has just arrived. Tabitha makes me eat my slices with a knife and fork, so as not to mess up my costume or makeup. Mom circles us, taking action shots with her big camera like the good photographer she is. She doesn't say anything about the new hue of my hair. It occurs to me that she probably assumes it was intentional, never suspecting that it's permanent.

After she's shot a roll of photos, Mom puts the camera away. Then she says, "No smoking, no drinking, no drug-taking. Hannah offered to pick you guys up at eleven on the dot. Don't keep her waiting, okay?"

I muster up a mock scowl. "Whatever happened to 'Have a good time'?"

Mom smiles and strokes a strand of my hair. "Have a good time, honey."

And on that note, we make our exit.

# Chapter 19

Tobin Scacheri lives in Abbey Road, a housing development in which every street is named after a Beatles song. His house is on the corner of Penny Lane and Revolution Way, and I can pick it out even before Hannah reads the correct number off the mailbox. It's a sprawling split-level, painted lavender with teal and salmon and lemon yellow trim, like something on *The Simpsons*. Exactly the kind of house I'd expect someone as cool as Tobin to live in.

Tabitha and I make our way up the long and winding driveway to the front door, and I tell her I think I'm going to be sick. "Oh, stop," she says. "You'll be fine." She presses the doorbell firmly, *bing*-bong. A striking woman dressed in full-on Gypsy garb answers the door. In her much-bejeweled hands she's holding a large plastic cauldron filled with candy. "I bet," she says, "you're here for the party?"

"Yes, ma'am," I say.

"Oh god," she groans, setting down the cauldron and snapping back her waist-length cape of chestnut hair. "When did *I* become a 'ma'am'? Please, call me

Claudia. Or at least Mom. And come in! It's so chilly tonight. Your poor legs must be freezing."

Before I can become officially embarrassed about the nakedness of my knees, I hear *his* voice: "Mom? Where'd you put the extra ginger ale?"

And then, like magic, he appears, wearing a short-sleeved tan button-down with matching shorts and worn leather hiking boots. He holds an inflatable pool toy shaped like an alligator in one hand and a large, mosquito-netted safari hat in the other.

"Hey," he says. "I was wondering when you two would show."

So much for the fashionable nature of being late. I flash Tabitha an I-told-you-so smirk.

"My son, the Crocodile Hunter," Claudia says, throwing her arms around Tobin and planting a loud kiss on his cheek.

"*Mom*, please."

Tobin wiggles away from her and pops the hat onto his head. "C'mon," he says. "Everybody's downstairs."

"Aren't you forgetting something?" Claudia asks. "How about some introductions?"

Tabitha automatically extends her hand to Tobin's mom. "Tabitha Donnelly," she says. "You have a beautiful home." Why can't I be that poised? Tobin's mom turns to me and says, "And you are . . . ?"

I open my mouth to answer but nothing comes out. Thankfully, Tobin touches my arm and says, "This is Lucy."

"Yes," I agree. "I'm Lucy."

"Lucy Pfefferminz!" Claudia claps her hands together, then throws them wide, like she's about to give me a hug. "You *are* adorable, aren't you?" She winks at Tobin, who, if I'm not mistaken, is actually blushing.

"It's Doyle, Mom," he says. "Lucy Doyle."

The corners of her mouth twist slightly, like she's thinking hard. "But there *is* a Pfefferminz, right? I know I've heard that name before."

Before I can figure out why Tobin's mom is so familiar with Lori Pfefferminz's name, the doorbell rings again, and Claudia glides back to the front door. While she dumps handfuls of Tootsie Rolls into the pillowcases of two Harry Potters and a Powerpuff Girl, Tobin shepherds us through the kitchen and down into the basement.

The room is dark, lit only by the dim glow of Christmas lights strung across the ceiling and a couple of Lava lamps. There are people *everywhere*, but otherwise, things seem relatively normal—music, sodas, snacks. Tobin steers us toward a couple of guys chowing down at the food table. He taps the one in army fatigues on the shoulder and says, "Hey, Spencer— there's someone you gotta meet." The boy turns around. A pair of Groucho gag glasses, the kind with the rubber nose and mustache, rest on his face, and two light-up devil horns poke from the top of his head. He takes one look at Tabitha's sequined horns and grins.

"Devil with a blue dress," he says, raising his cup to her. "All right."

"Let me guess." Tabitha bats her false eyelashes at him. "Devil in disguise?"

"You know it."

Tobin nods in Tab's direction. "Nice wig."

"Thanks," she says, keeping her eyes pasted on Spencer.

I'm looking at her looking at him, so the fact that Tobin Scacheri is fingering one of my newly shorn locks doesn't register right away.

"You cut your hair," he says.

"Yeah," I say.

"I thought it might be a wig like Tabitha's."

"No. All mine. Even the orange stripes."

Tobin's hand drops to my shoulder, setting off a series of small explosions inside my body. He asks me if I'd like some punch. "Don't worry," he says. "It's not spiked or anything." I still decline, hoping he won't, under any circumstances, remove that hand.

There's music playing in the background, and a trio of girls dressed like the members of Destiny's Child are demonstrating their enviable dancing skills. I think the one who's supposed to be Beyoncé Knowles is in my algebra class, but she's one of those freakishly beautiful people who don't even notice I exist. I really, really wish Allison had agreed to come. As I look around at the other faces, it occurs to me that with the exceptions of Tabitha and Beyoncé, I'm quite possibly the youngest person in the room.

If that's not scary enough, I spot Lori Pfefferminz shooting daggers at me from the other side of the basement. She's wearing a hot-pink *I Dream of Jeannie* getup that bares her perpetually tan stomach as well as showcases her more-than-generous cleavage. Still, it is *my* shoulder that Tobin has picked to place his hand on tonight.

But suddenly, the hand is gone, and Tobin drops to the floor, wrestling with his inflatable alligator. He beats it with his hat, whooping like a cowboy as he and the gator roll into the dance space. Everyone's cracking up, cheering him on. Tobin lifts his head and looks at me, but only for a second, like he's checking to see if I'm watching him, which of course I am. Then he dives onto the float with one final flop, effectively finishing the alligator off.

He stands and brushes some imaginary dirt from his shorts as applause breaks out.

Tobin rejoins us. Or rather, he rejoins *me*, since

Tabitha's abandoned my universe for Spencer's. He touches my arm, nodding in their direction. "I think he likes her."

"She has a boyfriend," I say.

"Oh yeah?"

"Yeah, but he's in New York."

Tobin nods. Then we just stand there, not talking, and I feel so completely awkward that I blurt out, "Lori Pfefferminz has a crush on you."

"I know."

"You do?"

"Yeah," he says. "But she's so . . . *obvious*. Not really my type."

I hear myself ask, "So what is your type?" But I'm not sure if this is in my head or something I actually say out loud because Tobin doesn't answer. Instead, he reaches into his pocket and pulls out a remote control. He aims it at the CD player, clicks a few buttons, and cues up an old Van Morrison song, "Tupelo Honey." I recognize it instantly because it's my parents' song, the one they first danced to at their wedding reception.

"This is a great song," I say.

"Dance with me?"

"Sure."

Tobin leads me to the center of the room. He takes my hands and places them on his shoulders, then puts his hands on my hips. We're so close that our knees are touching, but Tobin pulls me even closer. It's not so much dancing as it is hugging with movement. I wonder if he can feel the thump-thump of my heart against his delicious chest.

Spencer and Tabitha join us on the makeshift dance floor, as do a Dracula and a poor excuse for a Britney Spears. Tab catches my eye and mouths the words *You go*, and I just grin. But then I see Lori Pfefferminz, and she's scowling at me hard-core, and my grin disappears. Tobin must've seen her, too, because he takes my hand in his and discreetly pulls me behind a muslin sheet that acts as a door into what turns out to be the laundry room.

"Hi," he says, like we're meeting for the first time.

"Hi."

"God, you're cute," he says. And then, before the words can even register, Tobin Scacheri's mouth is mashed into mine, his tongue wiggling around inside, and he's finally kissing me, really kissing me, but all I can think about is the pain shooting through the lip lump Brody gave me earlier. It hurts so badly that I don't remember to kiss him back until the kiss is already over.

"I'm sorry," he says. "I thought you wanted me to kiss you."

"I did!" I say, far too loudly. Then again, softer: "I did. I just—"

"What?"

My eyes drop to the rust-colored carpeting. "I've never kissed anyone before. Not like that."

"Oh."

Why why *why* am I such an idiot? From the first time I saw Tobin Scacheri, all I've wanted is for him to kiss me, and then he does, and I have to go and ruin the entire thing. I stare at the floor, unable to look him in the eye.

"Did I hurt you?" Tobin asks, making me realize that I'm rubbing at the sore spot on my lip.

"Oh. No. I have this thing, this bruise—my little brother and I were kind of fighting earlier and, well, it *hurts*."

He laughs, and I'm feeling even more stupid when I feel two strong hands on my waist. Tobin lifts me up and places me on top of the washer. Then he moves his hands to either side of my face, pulls me close, and gently touches his lips to my lips.

"Better?" he whispers.

"Mmm."

He closes his eyes and kisses me again, soft at first, and then a little more firmly, but not so hard as to make the tender lump hurt more. Then his tongue finds its way back into my mouth, but it's different this time, not as wiggly. And then I start moving my tongue in his mouth and let my hands slip around his

147

shoulders. He moves his hands to the back of my head, and I can barely *breathe*, there's so much kissing.

The sheet guarding the laundry room rustles, and both of us freeze, like squirrels about to become roadkill. It's Lori Pfefferminz, calling Tobin's name. He places a finger over my lips, as if to shush me, and I don't know why I do it but I kiss his finger. He drops it to my chin, and he traces the line of my lower lip with his thumb.

"I think she's gone," he murmurs in my ear, and I'm about to be kissed again when the room is flooded with light. I blink away the blindness and see Lori in the doorway. She doesn't say a word, just glares at me, her hands planted on her hips. I try to jump down off the washing machine, but Tobin is so close I land on his feet, and we stand there, grasping each other like we're holding on for dear life.

The irritated snarl melts off Lori's face and is replaced with a little-girl pout. "There you are!" she says, sidling up to Tobin. She pokes one hot-pink fingernail at his chest and says, "Someone's not being a very good host, hiding out in here."

"I guess not," he says, blushing for the second time tonight. Then, very deliberately, Tobin Scacheri reaches out and laces his fingers through mine. "Lori, you know Lucy, right?"

Lori's eyelids narrow until they are little more than

paper-thin slits. "I don't think so," she says. "I don't hang out with *freshmen*."

I giggle, mostly out of nervousness, but also because she's so blatant in her Tobin lusting.

"What's so funny?" she asks.

"Nothing," I say. "I don't know. Aren't you friends with Kim Talbot?"

Lori tosses her ponytail. "That doesn't count—she's a cheerleader. We . . . cheer together."

"Oh, so that's what cheerleaders do," I deadpan, not quite sure where I'm getting this sudden gust of bravado.

Lori's face screws up like she's just taken a swig of sour milk. So much for sarcasm. As she quite visibly wracks her snotty little brain for an appropriate response, Tobin says, "We were just heading upstairs to get Lucy some . . . aspirin."

"Yeah," I chime in, catching on. "I have a headache."

"See you around," he says. He leads me through the sheet, across the basement, and up the stairs.

"Where are we going?" I ask.

"To get some aspirin."

I'm confused but follow him anyway, into this tiny half-bathroom with lime green walls and a black-and-white tiled floor, where he locks the door behind us.

"Hey, Tobin," I say, "I don't *really* have a headache."

"I know." Tobin smiles. We're still holding hands, and he starts massaging my thumb with his. My knees turn to tapioca.

But as Tobin closes his eyes and leans in for another kiss, I realize that I can't help thinking about stupid Lori and the incident that just took place. So I take a step backward and say, "Is there something between you and Lori Pfefferminz?"

"Not a thing. I mean, she likes me, but we never dated or anything."

He leans back in, but I put my palm square on his chest. "Is that all? She seems so possessive of you."

Tobin sighs. "I think I kissed her once. Over the summer. At some party."

"You *think* you kissed her?"

"I'd had a couple beers," he says. "But I don't do that stuff anymore. The drinking or the kissing of random girls, I mean. I always felt like such a jackass afterward."

"Oh. Well, why didn't you just say that to begin with?"

"Because it was nothing. And I don't know, I guess I was afraid it would sound like some lame excuse."

"My brother always says a lame excuse is better than no excuse at all."

"Yeah, that sounds right," he says. "I'm sorry."

I don't reply, so he continues, "I don't like Lori, Lucy, I like *you*. I want you to like me."

"But I do," I say. "I do like you."

"Really?"

I nod.

"Do you think—I mean, would it be okay if I kissed you again?"

"Yes," I say in a near whisper.

And so he does.

# Chapter 20

The rest of the party passes by in a blur. Tobin doesn't leave my side. He introduces me to a bunch of people and makes sure that neither of us comes close to Lori. I don't even *talk* to Tabitha until ten minutes before Hannah is scheduled to pick us up. Tab has spent most of the evening glued to Spencer, and though I never catch them kissing, they've traded horns by the time we have to go.

Tobin, ever the gentleman, insists on walking us out. In a stroke of impeccable timing, Hannah pulls up the second we step out Tobin's front door. Tabitha thanks Tobin for the invite and climbs into the van, but I linger.

"I'm glad you came," Tobin says.

"Me too."

He kisses me on my cheek. "See you at school."

"Yes," I say. "At school."

I get into the van and buckle my seat belt, a little bit puzzled by his comment. Aren't boys supposed to tell you that they'll call you, even if they never intend to? Still, I'm comforted by the fact that Tobin doesn't move. As Hannah drives away, he stands on the curb, following the van with his eyes. In fact, he's still watching us as we turn the corner.

Hannah's voice jolts me. "Have a good time?"

"It was okay," I say, not sure how much I should divulge in front of my brother's girlfriend, even if she seems really cool with that kind of stuff.

" '*Okay*'?" Tabitha practically shrieks. "Hannah, you should've seen her. She was practically floating."

"You should talk," I say, twisting around to face her. "Could you have possibly mooned over that Spencer guy any more?"

"Oh, that," she replies dismissively, "was harmless flirting."

"Looked like more than flirting to me."

"How could you tell, with your eyes locked on Tobin all night?" she retorts.

We give Hannah a quick recap of the party's highlights. Well, most of the highlights. I don't mention the washing machine, or the yummilicious kiss Tobin gave me in the lime green bathroom. Maybe I'll tell her later.

Tabitha and I do so much talking that I don't really notice Hannah's silence until after we've dropped Tab off. Hannah may be a lot of things, but quiet isn't one of them. I probably would've chalked it up to tiredness if I hadn't noticed a pasty, almost greenish look to her skin. And I probably would've attributed *that* to the glow of streetlights if Hannah hadn't been breathing so funky, sucking in great big lungfuls of air and letting them out slowly.

"You okay?" I ask.

"Mmm-hmm." She rolls the window down nearly all the way, inviting in an arctic blast of air.

"Isn't it a little cold for that?"

She doesn't answer, just pushes her curls off her face, which I realize is glistening slightly with sweat. Ever my mother's daughter, I put my hand on her forehead to check her temperature, but she's perfectly cool.

"Stop it," she says, pushing my hand away. I don't have time to get confused by the harshness of her tone, because suddenly the van swings violently to the right. Hannah slides the van into the breakdown lane, presses the hazard lights on, unsnaps her seat belt, and bolts from the car.

I whip around in my seat to look where Hannah's gone, but I can't see anything. I fling my door open and jump out into a soft dirt slope. In the blinking taillights I see Hannah hunched over, her back rising and falling almost convulsively. It takes a few beats for me to realize she's puking her guts up onto the faded asphalt of the road.

I stuff back my queasiness and rush to her side to help her keep her long hair from flying into the stream of vomit. The retching continues, and it sounds painful. When there's nothing left for her to heave, Hannah pants for a few minutes, croaks out a weak thanks, and straightens up. Then she starts walking back to the van like nothing happened.

"Are you okay to drive?"

"Yeah."

"Are you sure? Because I could call Mom on the cell phone and—"

"I'm *fine*," she says. "I just seem to get my morning sickness in the evening."

I do a double take as she eases the car back onto the road. Did she just say what I think she said?

"Yes," she says, without so much as a glance in my direction. "I am."

I sit in complete and utter shock as Hannah calmly reaches into the change cup for a loose piece of gum and pops it into her mouth. *"Pregnant."* The word ricochets through my brain. Without even thinking I say, "How did this *happen?*"

"Well," Hannah says, "It's like this: when a man and a woman love each other very much—"

"Come off it," I say. "You know what I mean."

She shifts the rearview mirror slightly. "Contraceptive failure," she says. "Either that or divine intervention. You choose." She takes a slow left onto Route 13. I don't think I've ever seen her drive so carefully.

"Does . . . does Jack know?"

She sighs. "Yes, of course."

"Mom?"

"Yeah."

"So what you're saying is I'm the only one who doesn't?"

"No," she says. "There's Brody."

"Yeah, but he's a *child*."

"So were you, the last time I checked."

I automatically roll my eyes, even though she can't see. "Whatever. I can handle these things, you know. I wish Mom would get a clue."

"Luce—this has nothing to do with your mom. Keeping it from you—that was all Jack."

"But why?"

We arrive at the house before she can answer. She puts the van in park and turns to me. "Look," she says. "I know I just dropped a big bomb on your head, and I'm sure you have a zillion questions for me. But here's the thing: you're not supposed to know yet. So we're going to go in, and you're going to tell your mom all about your fabulous party, and afterward we'll go up to your room and *then* we'll talk, okay?"

I nod and follow her up the steps. We find Mom in the den, half dozing in front of some black-and-white movie. "Hey," she says groggily when we've entered her line of vision. "How was it?"

"Fabulous," I say, swooping in to kiss her cheek. "G'night." Hannah shoots me a withering look.

"What was that?" Mom yawns, stretching her arms over her head.

"Very tired," I say, mimicking her yawn. "I'll tell you all about it over breakfast." I head upstairs, sure that Hannah will follow any second.

Only she doesn't. For at least ten minutes I wait to hear her bounding up the steps, but there's only silence.

Because I've just professed extreme tiredness and therefore cannot convincingly infiltrate the downstairs conversation, I distract myself by getting ready for bed. I'm not quite ready to lose the Tinker Bell garb, but I don't mind removing my makeup with a whopping smear of Noxzema. I chase that with a good, long session of Buff Puff-ing. It leaves my skin red but still freckled with the green and silver glitter that I'm beginning to think is now permanently welded to my face, neck, and arms.

Still no sign of Hannah. I run a brush through my hair, and as I do I think of Tobin Scacheri. The heat of his hand on the nape of my neck. The salty sweetness of his mouth. We *kissed*. My god, did we kiss. I conjugate the verb in my head: I kissed, he kissed, *we* kissed. I've been kissed. *Finally*.

I touch a finger to my bottom lip, still slightly sore

from all the kissing, or maybe it's from Brody clocking me this morning. Everything's become a blur; the Battle of the Brownie Batter feels like it happened a zillion years ago. And now—

Everything has changed.

# Chapter 21

It's exactly 12:15 A.M. by the time Hannah finally comes into my room.

"What took you so long?" I demand, tossing *The Scarlet Letter* aside.

Hannah closes her eyes, like it hurts to look at me. "Why aren't you asleep yet?"

"We're supposed to talk, remember?"

She drops gently to the foot of the bed that has become hers. "So what do you want to know?" she asks as she pulls off her sneakers and tosses them into a growing shoe pile in the corner.

I blink a few times, not sure which question to ask first. "Well," I say. "Why is this some big secret? I mean, you said it was an accident, but isn't it a happy one?" Hannah doesn't respond right away, and this silence tells me more than any answer she could offer. "Oh."

"Yeah," she says.

"So are you and Jack going to get married now?"

Hannah looks horrified. "God, no," she says. "I mean, don't get me wrong—I love your brother. But I'm not ready to get married. I want to finish school and start my career, and . . . and Jack . . . well, let's just say he's even less ready than I am."

She says this last thing more to herself than to me, but I hear it anyway. Her words make me feel slightly nauseated. Because it sounds like Jack's not gearing up to pass out bubble-gum cigars in a hospital waiting room. And I don't know, call me old-fashioned, but I'm kind of appalled that he didn't at least propose. It's not like they hate each other. They seem so much in love.

Then I recall the conversation I had with Mom right after they arrived. The one where Mom said that Jack was here to figure some things out and that Hannah was here because she was part of the package, "for now."

For now.

But not forever.

"You know what, Lucy? I feel kind of uncomfortable talking about this stuff. It wasn't my place to tell you to begin with—it just sort of came out."

"I just have one more question."

"Okay."

"I guess . . . I guess I want to know what happens now."

Hannah sighs, hugging a feather pillow to her chest. "You and me both."

Her back rises and falls like before, only more gently, and I think she's about to heave again until I realize she's crying. I don't know what to say, so I turn off all the lights and slip into the bed beside her. I wrap my arms around her shaking shoulders and tell her everything will be okay, and even though I doubt either of us believes the words, I think they make us both feel a little better.

When I wake up the next morning, Hannah is gone. Not just from the room, either; she's gone from the house. No note or anything. I ask Mom where Hannah went, but she just shrugs. "She probably went for a walk, Lucy. Give her some space."

I'm about to protest when Mom changes the subject. "Why don't you go wash that orange stuff out of your hair?"

Uh-oh.

"Great idea, Mom," I say weakly. "I'll get right on that."

But before I can figure out how I'm going to handle this latest hair debacle, the phone rings. It's Allison. "So how was it?" she asks eagerly. I take the cordless into the upstairs bathroom and fill her in on the disastrous party prep. "Yeah, yeah, yeah," she says. "Get to the juicier stuff."

"Like how Tobin kissed me?"

Allison shrieks so loudly that I think my eardrums will pop. *"I can't believe you had your first kiss with Tobin Scacheri!"*

The other line beeps. "Hold that thought," I say, and click over.

"Hey, Tink," Tabitha says. "Was that some party or what?"

I ask her to hold on, then click back to Allison. "Hey, can I call you back?"

"Sure," Allison says. "Who is it? Is it *Tobin?*"

"No," I say. "It's Tabitha."

"Oh." She sounds disappointed. "Well, yeah. Definitely call me back."

I promise her I will, then click back to Tabitha, who promptly begins recounting last night's festivities at warp speed: "Lori Pfefferminz was mad. Did you see that? Do you think Spencer's cute? He asked for my number. Do you think he'll call me? Do I even want him to call me? I can't tell Elliot, 'cause he'd be so jealous. But maybe that's a good thing. I don't know. Hey, too bad Tobin didn't kiss you last night—"

"But he did," I interject. "He kissed me many, many times."

For a whole fifteen seconds, Tabitha is speechless. Then she starts bombarding me with questions:

"When? How did it happen? Was he a good kisser? It wasn't too wet, was it? Those are the worst."

"Whoa," I say. "Slow down, Tabitha. You sound like the girl from that video we watched in health—you know, the one who was taking all those diet pills."

Tabitha laughs. "No diet pills for me. But I did have four cups of coffee this morning."

Before I can tell her she should switch to decaf, the call waiting beeps again. "I should answer that," I say. "It might be Tobin."

But it's not Tobin, it's Allison. Again.

"You're taking too long," Allison complains. "And Tabitha was there. I'm the one who needs details."

So then I tell Tabitha I'll have to call *her* back. But about thirty seconds into my conversation with Allison, the line beeps *again*. "If it's anyone other than Tobin," Allison commands, "you better ditch them."

"Are you going out with Tobin Scacheri now?" an unfamiliar voice says, without the courtesy of a simple hello.

"Who is this?"

"Kim. Kim Talbot."

"Oh." Figures.

"So are you?"

"I don't know," I say.

"What do you mean you don't know? Either you're dating or you aren't."

"I told you, I don't know. He . . . he gives me rides home from school. And last Tuesday he took me to Battery Park, and he said something about taking me to a museum where his mom works."

"Ugh," she says. "Who'd want to go there? But at least it's a date. Yeah, I'd say he's your boyfriend."

The constant beeping continues for at least another hour before I am allowed to retire from the phone. Still, each time it rings I am certain it will be Tobin Scacheri, who, despite the six assurances of my trusty Magic 8 Ball, never does call.

Tired of the incessant talking, Mom takes the phone off the hook around three; I'm secretly glad, not only because I'm starting to get tired of dishing up the details of Tobin's and my mouth mash, but also because said mouth masher *still* has not called. Without the constant ringing, the house is eerily quiet. Brody is off at Stu's house, Mom's in her darkroom developing the sixteen roles of film she shot of us in our costumes, and Hannah is still god-knows-where. So it's just me, really, curled up in the den, trying to plow through *The Scarlet Letter*. Which is sort of impossible, since all I can think about is Hannah, and how thank god she doesn't have to wear a scarlet anything attached to her chest. Actually, I only think this for a minute before getting sidetracked by what letter Hannah would have to wear, since technically she's not an adulterer. I am contemplating "F," as in "fornicator," when Hannah herself walks through the front door.

I bolt upright. "Where have you been?"

"Out."

"Out where?"

Hannah shrugs off her hot-pink velour jacket. "I had a job interview," she says.

"For eight hours?"

She doesn't answer. Instead, she hands me a bulging Happy Harry's Drugstore bag. "I picked these up for you."

Inside, I find five different shades of hair dye, running the spectrum from platinum to ebony. "What am I supposed to do with these?"

"Pick one," she says. "I figured you'd want something to get rid of the orange."

"Thanks."

Hannah flops into my dad's chair, this beaten-up monstrosity upholstered in orange-and-navy plaid. She lets her head roll to the side a bit, so it's resting on her shoulder, and she looks so little and fragile, I'm almost afraid to speak. Almost.

"So where was your interview?" I ask in my softest voice.

Without opening her eyes, she murmurs, "The Food-n-Stuff. You're looking at their newest cashier."

"Congratulations."

"Don't," she says. "I mean, I appreciate the effort, but it's not like I'm achieving some lifelong career goal."

"Then why take it?"

"Because it starts at seven fifty an hour, and the union requires them to give me benefits right away," she says. "I'm too old to be on my mom's health insurance."

"Oh."

She rubs her eyes open. "I'm at the end of my first trimester. I can't afford all the wellness exams and checkups out of pocket. Jack and I don't even have enough saved to buy a month's worth of diapers yet, let alone full-on medical care."

"*Oh.*"

Hannah reaches for the Happy Harry's bag. "So, what will it be?" She grins, looking more like her usual self, and holds up two of the dye boxes. "Marilyn Monroe or Lucille Ball?"

"You don't have to do this," I say.

"I know."

She turns her attention back to the contents of the bag and fishes out the box of ebony dye. "Now, I know this is a stretch, and your mom will probably freak, but with your light eyes and fair skin—"

"Hey," I say. "Are you . . . are you okay?"

Her hand tightens around the box. "I'm fine."

"Jack will be home soon."

"Yeah," she says. "Thank god for small miracles."

"When was the last time you talked to him?"

"Four nights ago." Hannah gathers up the boxes, signaling the end of that conversation. We head to the upstairs bathroom, where she talks me into the ebony. I don't know how she does it, but she does. Then she hands me a box of dark red henna and says, "My turn." When we've finished coating each other's heads in smelly goop, we tie plastic bags over our hair and take turns blasting ourselves with Hannah's trusty blow dryer.

And this is how both of us avoid dealing with the Big Things hanging over our space, like heavy clouds about to burst into rain.

The phone rings at eight P.M., and I'm caught off guard because the last I knew, it was still off the hook. I pounce on it, certain that this time it *is* Tobin, who's been going out of his mind wondering why my line has been busy since this afternoon. But I'm even more relieved to hear my brother's voice on the other end of the line.

"Jack? Where are you?"

"Toronto. Is Hannah there?"

"Why are you in Toronto? I thought you'd be back this way, not going farther north."

"Don't start with me, Lucy."

"I think you should come home, Jack."

His voice grows thin. "Get. Hannah. Okay?"

"But—"

"Goddammit, Lucy!" Jack bellows. "Will you put her on the phone?"

I walk the cordless over to Hannah, who's staring into Martha's dark cage like it's some extraordinary movie she's thoroughly engrossed in. "It's Jack," I say. I hand the phone off gently, as if it were a bomb about to explode in my fingers.

"Hey, you," Hannah says. She doesn't ask me to leave the room, but I do anyway, because I certainly do not want to be present when Jack tells her that he's now in another country.

I wander into the kitchen, where I find Mom at her usual post, sipping her regular cup of chamomile and trying to solve her latest crossword puzzle. She glances up at me, and her mouth flies open in shock. "Please tell me that's a wig."

My hair. I reach up and tuck a chunk of it behind my ears. "It's not," I say. "It's . . . permanent." And I guess my face looks strange because she says, "Oh, honey," in a voice that makes me want to cry.

Mom motions for me to come to her, which I do, and she puts her arms around me so tightly that I'm practically falling into her lap. "It's only hair," she says. "It'll grow out."

I shake my head. "This isn't about my stupid *hair*."

"Then what's wrong?"

"Jack and Dad are in Toronto."

"Toronto?" she repeats, confused. "I don't remember anything about Toronto."

"Exactly."

"Oh," she says, finally getting it. Then again: "*Oh*."

"Things," I say, "are about to become really, really ugly."

# Chapter 22

Back in my room, I try to distract myself by plucking through my clothes to see if I've got any that will go with my new hair. I've just about emptied my entire closet when Hannah ambles in, her big cat eyes turned acid green from what I suspect is a whole lot of crying.

"What are you doing?" she asks, sniffling and surveying the clothes-heaped disaster that has become our bedroom.

"Looking for something to wear," I admit, too afraid to ask her how the conversation with Jack went.

Hannah nods, then throws open her red plastic suitcase, fishes out a faux-suede cheetah-print miniskirt, and tosses it to me. Then she procures a square-necked black sweater with three-quarter sleeves. "You have black tights, right?" she says while pawing through a pile of scarves. I nod. She plucks out a sheer square of fabric the same pattern as the skirt and hands it to me. "Wear it in your hair," she says. "Knot it underneath, not on top."

"Thanks," I say.

"No problem." I watch as Hannah snatches various

items: a pair of pj's, her pink fuzzy bunny slippers, a purple notebook. "I'm sleeping downstairs," she informs me, and leaves before I can even say good night.

Brody wanders into the kitchen as I'm trying to choke down my breakfast the next morning and starts making jokes about my new hair color, asking me if I fell in an oil slick, ha ha ha. I keep gnawing my way through a partially toasted frozen waffle, too busy worrying about Hannah to properly defend myself. The waffle is cold and slimy and making me feel nauseated. I spit a lump of it into my napkin and throw the rest of it away.

Out of nowhere, the doorbell rings. *Jack did come home!* I think. *He'll know how to fix things.* I'm so excited by the prospect that I throw open the door without first checking the peephole.

"Jesus!"

"Nah, it's just me." Tobin Scacheri grins, reaching forward to finger a lock of my hair. "You changed it again."

"What are you doing here?"

"Well," he says. "I thought maybe you'd want a ride to school."

Mom calls out from the kitchen, "Lucy, who are you talking to?"

Tobin booms, "That would be me, Mrs. Doyle."

"Who's 'me'?" she replies, striding into the foyer. She sees Tobin and stops.

"Hi," he says. "I'm Tobin. Tobin Scacheri."

"The boy with the party." Her eyes narrow slightly. "How old are you?"

"Mom!"

"I just turned seventeen."

She doesn't break her gaze. "When?"

"Three months ago."

Could she be any more embarrassing? "Tobin's going to give me a ride to school," I say. "Is that okay?" I grab my backpack off the floor before she can protest.

"Wear your seat belt," she says. Then she turns to Tobin and offers a weak smile. "Nice to meet you."

"Yeah, you too."

Tobin keeps a safe distance from me as we walk down the steps. Mom watches us from the doorway. He opens my door and closes it after I've slid into the newly patched seat. I sneak a peek at Mom. She approves.

We pull away; the engine purrs at a volume only slightly louder than that of a normal car. Tobin says, "She sounds good, doesn't she?"

"Yeah."

Then he says, "Did I just get you into trouble?"

"I don't think so."

"Your mom looked . . . I don't know. Not completely happy."

"She—she was surprised," I stammer. "Anyway, I don't think it's you she's mad at. There's been a lot going on."

"Like what?"

I really don't feel like telling Tobin Scacheri that my brother not only got his secret girlfriend pregnant but can't deal with the idea of being a father. I mean, it's just too much. So instead, I say breezily, "You know . . . stuff." He nods like he understands, but at the next stoplight, he looks at me like he's waiting for me to say more. When I don't, he flips on the radio and hums along.

Time to change the subject. "I had a good time at your party." I say. He gives me one of those smiles, the kind that throws my heartbeat into a syncopated rhythm, and says, "Me too." There is genuine heat radiating from his elbow to my own. Tobin's body is leaning right and mine is leaning left, like we can't bear to be even six inches apart from one another. The only boys I've ever sat this close to are my brothers, and I'm fairly certain that their elbows don't do anything all that special.

We pull into the junior/senior parking lot. Tobin cuts the engine, but neither of us gets out. His hand lands on my forearm, and I stare at it, wondering where it will go next. I feel his face getting closer to mine, but I don't look up. "Lucy," he says in a gentle voice. I draw a sharp breath, and before I can let it out, Tobin's mouth is latched on to mine.

I remember an old *Brady Bunch* rerun where Bobby kisses this girl who has the mumps—Millicent, I think. And I remember thinking how stupid it was that he imagined fireworks going off. But this is how I feel when Tobin kisses me. *Explosive.* Like all of these little fizz-pops are going off inside my body, and there's nothing I can do to control them.

# Chapter 23

There is a vibe buzzing through Haley High, a me-and-Tobin vibe. We walk the halls, Tobin's hand placed on the center of my back as if to say, *We're together*. You can almost hear some funk-style theme music trailing us as we part the sea of student bodies, Moses style.

He escorts me to homeroom, but I don't go in right away, because Tobin Scacheri kisses me, right there, in front of everybody. It's not a big kiss, more of a series of soft, lingering pecks, but I'm still caught off guard—it is, after all, our first official Public Display of Affection. The pecks don't stop, and eventually I forget where I am and become conscious only of the kissing itself. The first warning bell rings.

"Meet me after school?" Tobin asks, combing a finger through my hair.

"Sure."

He delivers one last, quick kiss to my mouth, then sprints down the hall toward his own homeroom. I watch him run, still feeling all wobbly in the knees. So *this* is what it's like. Sighing, I retreat to my desk and calculate just how many minutes until I'll see Tobin again.

At lunch, Allison and I are dissecting the Tobin situation for about the millionth time when Tabitha suddenly appears. I have no idea how the girl manages to sneak out of class so effortlessly.

"Can't stay long," she says. "But I just ran into Spencer and he wants to know if you and Tobin want to come with us to the planetarium Saturday night."

"What, are you guys *dating* now?" Allison asks.

Tabitha shrugs. "I guess it's a date."

"What about Elliot?" I say.

"What *about* Elliot?" she says. "He's in New York. It's not like *he* can take me to the planetarium on Saturday night."

"Yeah, but—" I start.

"Let it go, okay?" Tabitha snaps. "So. Saturday?"

"What's at the planetarium?"

"Laser show. They're doing a tribute to some musician who shot himself."

"Sounds like fun," Allison says.

At first, I think she's just being sarcastic. But then she says, "Do you know how much it costs? My babysitting funds are running seriously low." Tabitha and I exchange looks, which Ally of course picks up on. "What?" she asks. "Am I not invited?"

"It's not that," Tabitha says smoothly. "It's just—"

"Cars," I say. "Tobin's car only seats four."

I'm being lame and I know it. But I *am* new at this dating thing, and I guess I never would've pegged Allison as a fifth-wheel type of person.

"Never mind," she says, clearly irritated. She crumples her milk pouch into a tight ball and rises, even though lunch isn't half over. "I have . . . stuff to do. See you later."

Tabitha sighs as Allison stomps off. "Well, *that* was awkward."

"Yes," I agree, a tiny pocket of guilt forming in my already churning stomach.

Tobin drives me home after school, and I invite him in. We're kissing in the foyer when I hear my mother's voice call out, "Luce? Is that you?" Tobin pulls away abruptly.

"Should I leave?" he asks.

I tell him no and we head into the kitchen. My mother looks up from the table. "Oh," she says. "I didn't realize you had company."

"Hi, Mrs. Doyle." Tobin gives her a little wave.

177

She smiles. "Hello, Tobin. Please, call me Abby." He nods, and his shoulders lose some rigidity. Then she says, "I'd offer you a snack, but Lucy and I have some things we need to discuss."

Tobin nods again. "Sure, I, um, was about to take off anyway."

"I'll walk you out," I say.

"Just a minute." Mom stands and walks toward Tobin. She says, "I was wondering if you would like to come to dinner tomorrow night."

A flash of total panic crosses Tobin's face. Or maybe I'm just projecting. At any rate, it takes him a few seconds to find his smile. Eventually, he says, "I'd like that, Mrs. . . . Abby."

Mom laughs a nice, easy laugh. "Mrs. Abby is very glad that Mr. Tobin has accepted her invitation. Why don't you plan on six? Or earlier, if that works better for you."

I walk Tobin to his car. "I think she likes me," he says. "Do you think she likes me?"

"*I* like you," I say shyly, but for the first time, *I'm* the one to kiss *him*.

I practically float back into the kitchen, but then I see Mom. She doesn't look happy. In fact, the little wrinkle between her eyebrows is actually twitching.

"You should sit," she says gently.

I sit.

Mom pushes her bangs out of her eyes. She says nothing at first, and this makes me nervous. Why would she invite Tobin to dinner if she was going to tell me I'm not allowed to date him?

Finally, she speaks. "There's no easy way to say this, so I might as well just do it. Here's the thing, Luce—"

"Is this about Tobin?"

"What? No. No, Tobin seems like a nice boy. But that's not what I wanted to talk to you about. It's . . . Hannah."

"Oh god," I say. "Did something happen to the baby?"

Mom's eyes fly open. "Excuse me?"

*Oops.*

"Mom—I know. About the baby."

"Clearly." She lets out a large breath. "Well."

"Is that all you wanted to tell me?"

"No."

"No?"

Mom fiddles with the salt and pepper shakers. They're shaped like Dutch windmills, and the mill parts actually spin. She flicks at the spinners, *flick flick flick.*

"Uh, Mom?"

"Right," she says. "This must be sort of a shock for you. We can talk about it, if you like. We probably should. Talk."

I resist the urge to roll my eyes. "I know where babies come from. We had that talk years ago, remember?"

"That's not what I mean. I just think . . . well, I know how much you look up to Jack."

"So?"

"So this must be confusing for you. Isn't it?"

I shrug. "I don't know."

Mom reaches across the table and squeezes my hand. "Come on, Luce. Throw me a bone here. I need to know what you're thinking. I need to know you're okay."

"But I don't know what I think," I say. "On the one hand, it's kind of exciting that there's this little person on the way. But then it's so weird to think of Jack being a dad." Mom nods, so I take a deep breath and continue. "I guess the only thing I'm really worried about is . . . well, Hannah, actually. I get the sense that Jack doesn't really want to be a dad. He doesn't, does he?"

She shakes her head. "I don't know, honey."

"Everything will be okay, though, won't it?" I say. "He'll come home and get a job, and then when they've saved enough money, they'll get a little apartment of their own. And I can baby-sit sometimes, on weekends."

Mom frowns. "Is that what Hannah said?"

"Well, no. I guess I just assumed that's what would happen—why they're here."

She takes a deep breath, lets it out slowly. "It's a bit more complicated than that, honey."

"What do you mean?"

"Hannah's mother thinks it would be best for Hannah to go stay with her for a while."

"But what about Jack?"

"Jack could decide to go to California with her. Or he could decide to stay here, or even go back to school. So could Hannah, for that matter. Eventually."

Suddenly I realize why my mother asked me to sit. This situation is far more serious than I thought. I mean, it's one thing to deal with the fact that in six short months my brother will be the parent of a teeny tiny baby. But it's an entirely different thing to think of him completely abandoning said baby.

"So what happens to Hannah? She can't work at the Food-n-Stuff forever. She wants to finish school—she told me."

Mom lets out a soft sigh. "I know this might be difficult for you to understand, but Hannah had a choice, and she chose to have her baby. Becoming a mother is a wonderful thing, but it also shifts the focus of your life. Believe me, no one thinks Hannah's new job is ideal. We're all just trying to figure out the best plan for her and the baby. So yes, that might mean Hannah puts her own needs on hold. For a little while, anyway."

"That's what Jack needs to do, too, then, right? Did you tell him that?"

"Jack's my son," she says slowly. "But he's also twenty years old. I can't force decisions on him, no matter how much I may want to."

"But you don't think he'll break up with her, do you? I mean, why would he? Hannah is so awesome, and they seem like they're so much in love."

She smiles warmly. "There's a big difference, Luce, between being in love and building a life together. You can be ready for one without being ready for the other. Sort of like how you might be ready to start dating, but you are nowhere near ready to start having sex. *Any* kind of sex."

"Mother!" I feel my cheeks grow hot; they must be turning eight shades of red.

"I read these stories, Lucy . . . about girls your age doing things I couldn't even imagine doing when I was in college, let alone when I was a freshman in high school."

"Yeah, but I'm not one of them."

"I know, honey. And I'm not trying to say that I think you're going to hop into bed with the first boy who tells you you're pretty. What I am saying is this: if you feel like you're ready, I hope you feel like you can talk to me. Even if it's tomorrow—and god, I hope it's not—but even if it is, I want you to come talk to me. I can't promise I'll be happy about it, but I won't get angry, either. Your health and well-being mean everything to me."

"Thanks," I say. I mean it, too. Sometimes I forget how cool my mother actually is. I can't imagine what it must be like for Tabitha. I'm quite certain her mother never gave her this speech.

"So do you have any questions for me?" Mom asks.

"Not about that. Not yet."

"Okay."

We sit quietly for a few minutes. Mom goes back to spinning the windmills. After a while I say, "So what are we going to do?"

"There's not much we can do," she says. "Anyhow, nothing's definite yet. From what I can tell, Hannah won't make any moves until Jack gets back. So I guess we'll have to wait and see."

"Where *is* Jack?"

"Toronto."

"No," I say. "Why isn't he here? He should be here."

She smiles. "They need the money." Mom places the windmills back on their wooden stand. "I think it's good for them, actually. Him being gone. It sort of gives Hannah a preview of what their future might be like together."

"How so?"

"Honey, I love your father. I don't regret a single moment we've been with each other. But I'll tell you this: I never pictured spending half my life as a jazz widow. And Jack . . . well, he's his father's son."

Of course, as soon as she says the words, they make total sense. I guess I'm so used to Dad being away that I never really considered what it does to Mom. I've never once heard her complain.

Mom swallows hard and rubs her temple with the base of her hand. She looks like she's in need of a dose of chamomile—or maybe a couple of glasses of wine. I reach across the table and squeeze *her* hand. "It's going to be okay," I say.

"Hey, that's my line."

"I know," I say. "But you looked like you needed to hear it more."

# Chapter 24

There's a weird sort of melancholy filling up the house tonight. For one thing, no one's here, because Hannah's pulling her first shift at the Food-n-Stuff and Brody is eating at Stu's. Ordering pizza was Mom's suggestion, and since it's just the two of us, we eat in the den, watching *Jeopardy!* It's a celebrity edition, so the questions are completely mindless, but neither of us shouts answers at the screen like we normally do. In fact, Mom doesn't say anything, even when I accidentally squirt a big blob of sauce onto the carpet.

After dinner, I go up to my room, exchange the clothes Hannah lent me for a pair of Polarfleece pj's, and crawl into my bed. My head throbs like there's a little man inside it, tapping his hammer at all the sensitive spots of my skull. Or like the words swimming inside me are really high-powered Ping-Pong balls: "brother," "baby," "boyfriend." I pull the covers far over my head but it's no use. I can't make my brain be quiet.

Eventually I give up and decide to call Allison. I still haven't told anyone about what's going on with Hannah and Jack, and really, she *is* my best friend.

"Honey, I'm sorry," Mrs. Ziegler says. "But Allison doesn't want to talk to you right now."

So much for tact.

I'm too emotionally exhausted to put up a fight, so I thank her, shamefaced, and immediately dial Tabitha's line. The phone rings about forty times, but I'm so spaced out that I don't realize no one's answering. Finally, I snap to and am ready to hang up when a tearful Tabitha whimpers hello.

"Tab? What's wrong?"

She sniffles. "Can I call you back? I'm on the other line."

"Sure," I say. "But, just tell me—are you okay?"

"Sort of," she says. "I'll call you later."

She hangs up before I can press for more, which is fine by me. I'm too wrapped up in my own drama to deal with someone else's. Of course, thinking this makes me feel like the worst friend *ever*, so I shed the comfy pj's, throw on some clothes, and head back downstairs.

"Where are you going?" Mom asks from her perch in the den.

"I'm going to bike over to Tabitha's," I say. "She sounds kind of messed up."

"About?"

"I don't know—that's why I'm going over there."

She arches one of her eyebrows. "Don't you have homework?"

"No," I lie, stuffing my feet into an old pair of Nikes.

Mom nods. "Wear your helmet. And be home by eleven."

I shove my key into my pocket and slip out the door. It's cold and windy, but I zip through the mile-long ride anyway.

I park my bike at the mailbox, strapping the helmet to the handlebars. I don't bother with the lock. Our neighborhood isn't the ritziest, but I've never had to worry about anything getting stolen. I go up to the door and knock; Tabitha answers, her nose bright red from crying. "Hey," she says. "What are you doing here?"

"Checking on you."

She motions me inside, and we go up the stairs to her bedroom. It's filled with a soft pinkish glow, courtesy of the small seashell lamp on her night table. Tabitha drops to the carpet and I follow suit, careful to steer clear of the crumpled tissues that dot the floor like half-melted snowballs.

"So are you going to tell me what's wrong?"

She sighs heavily. "It's Elliot," she says. "We broke up."

"Oh god," I say. "I'm so sorry."

"Yeah, well." She blows her nose into a half-used tissue, then tosses it across the room. "You think you're prepared for this, you know? And then it happens, and it's like, *whomp*, you can't even deal."

I pluck a fresh tissue from the box beside me and hand it to her. "I can't believe he did it over the phone. Jack always says a real man should do it face to face."

"But Luce—" Tabitha says. "I broke up with *him*."

"*What?* Why? Because of Spencer?"

"Not really," she says. "It's because the whole thing got so stupid. He lives three hours away, he doesn't have a car, and he certainly can't afford bus fare on a regular basis. I'm not the kind of person who thrives on tragedy, you know?"

"Then why are you so upset?"

"Because it hurts," she says, her eyes filling up with new tears. "I can't believe how much it hurts."

"If it hurts so much, then why end it?"

"Just because something *has* to be over doesn't mean you *want* it to be over."

I am reeling, literally reeling. My back sinks into the hot-pink shag carpeting and I cover my eyes with my hands.

"Lucy, get up. Lord, you'd think I'd just dumped *you*."

"But what about all that talk about feeling like he's your reality? What about that?"

"Don't yell at me."

"I'm not," I say. "It's just . . . well . . . you *slept* with him."

"So?"

"So how can you . . . you know . . . just end it like nothing ever happened?"

"Sex, Lucy," Tabitha says quietly. "We had sex. You can say the word."

"That's not the point."

"Then what *is* the point?"

"The point is," I say, "you gave him your *virginity*. Didn't this other stuff occur to you then?"

Tabitha's posture automatically corrects itself. "What's that supposed to mean?"

"It's just . . ." I pick at a piece of loose rubber flapping off the sole of my sneaker. "Well, sex is so huge, you know? Or at least, it's supposed to be. Isn't it?" Tabitha nods. I realize I'm walking a fine line here and that I need to choose my words carefully. "I guess I always thought I wouldn't do that with someone unless I was in love with that person. And if I *were* in love with a person enough to want to be with them—to want to have . . . sex . . . with them—then I wouldn't stop being in love with them so quickly. You know?"

"But I did love him. I mean, I thought I loved him."

She shakes her head. "It felt right, Lucy. I *wanted* to do it."

"But what if you had gotten pregnant? And then woke up two days later and realized you were never in love to begin with? Or worse, what if the guy who got you pregnant was acting like Jack?"

"What does Jack have to do with this?"

I take a deep breath. "Hannah's pregnant."

"She's *what?*"

"Pregnant," I say. "But you can't tell anyone. I mean, Brody doesn't even know yet."

"Oh my *god*," she says. "I can't believe Jack's going to be a—" Tabitha's fingers fly to her mouth.

"Father," I finish for her. "I know."

We stare at each other across the foot of floor space between us. Finally, Tabitha says, "Are they keeping it?"

"Yeah."

"Intense."

"There's more," I say. "Hannah's mom wants her to move back to California."

"Makes sense, I guess," Tabitha says. "Do you think she will? Would Jack go with her if she did?"

I shake my head. "I don't know. Everyone keeps giving me these wishy-washy answers. But I kind of get the feeling that's not what Jack wants. The baby, I mean—not just California."

We're quiet for a moment. Then Tabitha says, "We used a condom. I insisted."

I shrug. "Hannah was on the pill and she still got pregnant."

Tabitha rolls her eyes. "I don't need lectures, Lucy. I get enough of those from Nunzio."

"I know that," I say. "But weren't you the one sitting at my kitchen table like two weeks ago, bawling your eyes out because you thought maybe Nunzio was right to call you a slut?"

"Is that what you think?" she shrills.

"I didn't say that! I just—"

"You're just thinking it, right? Because girls who do it are bad people. Boys get high-fived by their fathers, but whatever. I didn't do anything wrong."

"I didn't say you did. Honest, Tabitha."

"Whatever." She looks down at the carpet, rubbing the ends of her hair so furiously I'm surprised they don't catch fire. "So are you psyched about Saturday?"

"Sort of," I say, grateful for the change in conversation. "I feel bad about ditching Allison."

"Yeah, me too."

"She's not talking to me, you know. At least, she wouldn't talk to me tonight."

Tabitha shrugs. "She'll get over it."

"Maybe."

"It's different, you know," she says. "After you've done it, it's harder to relate to girls who haven't."

Her words make me feel, once again, like I am so far behind the learning curve, I'll never catch up. Then again, I'm not even sure I want to.

"I don't mean you," she adds quickly. "But at least you're *dating*. I mean, I like Allison and all. But it's so much easier to talk to you."

I nod; even though Tabitha's reasoning doesn't make much sense—she confided in me about Elliot well before Tobin's mouth ever met mine—I think I know what she means now. Lately I've felt closer to Tabitha than Ally, and I have a strong suspicion it has to do with the boy thing. I think about the talk Allison and I had just a few weeks ago, about how strange everything had become, what with the Kims and Tabitha letting their respective boyfriends start to round the bases (or in Tab's case, hit a home run). But now it's different. Now I'm on the other side of the line.

And the truth is, I think I like it better over here.

# Chapter 25

I leave Tabitha's around quarter to eleven, rushing home so that I don't break curfew. I park my bike out back; Hannah's fumbling with her key when I return to the front door. Apparently Mom forgot to leave the porch light on before going to bed. "Hi," I say, relieving her of an enormous trash bag filled with god-knows-what. "Did you just get off work?"

"Yeah," she grunts, finally popping the door. "What's your excuse?"

"Nursing a broken heart."

"Not yours, I hope."

"No," I say. "Tabitha's. Hey, what's in this thing? It weighs a ton."

Hannah shoots straight for the den, flopping into the comfy chair. "They're for you," she says. "I took a little trip to the Salvation Army on my dinner break."

I dump the contents of the bag onto the floor and discover a heaping mound of clothes: three corduroy A-line micro-miniskirts, a handful of cotton button-downs with three-quarter sleeves, two pristine pairs of black capris, more turtlenecks than I care to count. I look up, wide-eyed. "How could you afford all this?"

"They were selling stuff by the pound—trying to make room for everyone's Christmas castoffs, I guess." Hannah leans forward, poking through the pile. She extracts a pair of silver lamé skinny pants and says, "I guess I got a little silly toward the end, huh?"

I shake my head, marveling over a small, squared-off purse with a half-moon-shaped handle. When I open it, I find a strand of fake pearls, a handful of earrings, and a pair of cat's-eye sunglasses, the kind with rhinestones embedded in the flared edges. "This stuff is amazing," I say.

Hannah smiles. "There are some shoes, too—check out the Mary Janes."

"Are these Doc Martens? Tabitha's going to drool herself a lake."

"So I did good then?"

I spring up and throw my arms around her neck. "Better than good," I say. "You're the best."

After patiently enduring more of my overenthusiastic thanks, Hannah disentangles herself from my limbs. "Time for bed," she says. "It's almost midnight."

We gather up my new wardrobe and transfer it to the bedroom. Hannah hits the bathroom as I sort the items into small laundry piles, extracting an outfit for tomorrow. When she returns, she says, "So why was Tabitha's heart broken?"

"She and the New York boy broke up."

"Ouch."

"The weird thing is, she broke up with him." I pause. "It got me thinking about some stuff."

"Yeah?" Hannah wraps a velvet hair band around her tangle of curls. "What about?"

"Like what I'll say if Tobin Scacheri decides he wants to sleep with me."

"Oh." She lets out a big breath, and my face gets hot. I can't believe I blurted it out like that. I feel like a complete idiot.

Her voice startles me. "He's not pressuring you or anything, is he?"

"God, no. We haven't even gone a real date. It's just . . . he's older. And it might come up."

Hannah nods. "So have you?"

"Have I what?"

"Figured out what you'll say."

I shake my head. "I guess 'no' is a little simplistic, huh?"

"It's a good start," she says. "But what happens if you're not feeling like you're in a very 'no' kind of place?"

If I wasn't blushing twenty-seven shades of red before, I certainly am now. "What do you mean?" I say, knowing full well what she means.

Hannah tosses me a look that calls me on my innocent act. "There's a reason girls have sex, Lucy. And it's not just because their friends are, or because their cute older boyfriends threaten to break up with them if they don't."

"Tobin isn't like that," I say.

"Probably not. But you should think about what you want."

Hannah pulls back the covers and slips into her bed, signaling the end of the conversation, at least for her. I go to brush my teeth; when I return, all the lights are out. I climb into my own bed. The numbers on my digital alarm clock tell me it's 12:28, but I'm not even close to being sleepy. I toss and turn, thrashing about the mattress long enough to prompt Hannah to ask me if I'm battling the boogeyman under my comforter. I click on my bedside lamp.

She groans, blinking back the light. "What's up, Luce?"

"I can't sleep."

"Does that mean I can't, either?"

I pretend not to hear that. "I was just wondering how old you were."

"Twenty. Can we turn out the light now?"

"No," I say. "I mean, how old were you the first time you . . . you know." Why is it so impossible for me to say the word "sex"? Hannah groans again, then says, "Can't we talk about this in the morning?"

"I have school in the morning."

"How about after school?"

"Tobin's coming over then. Mom invited him for dinner."

"Maybe he's the one who should practice saying no to you." She sighs. "I was fifteen."

"Was he your first love?"

Hannah snorts. "Not exactly. He was this gorgeous theater brat at my mom's school. She always let me go to the cast parties. I flirted with him all night, he fed me the requisite amount of champagne, and one thing led to another."

"So what happened?"

"That's pretty much it, babe."

"Oh."

We're quiet. For a minute I think Hannah's trying to fall back asleep, even though the lights are still on, but when I don't hear any deep breathing, I say, "Were you glad you did it?"

"I don't think 'glad' is the right word. . . . At the time I felt like I was winning some sort of prize—you know, snagging the hot older boy all the college girls wanted. And it was fine. I wasn't traumatized by it or anything. But sometimes I wish my first time hadn't been so . . . I don't know. Clinical."

Suddenly I wish I hadn't started this line of conversation. I mean, I'm glad Hannah's being honest with me. But I didn't expect her to be *so* honest.

"So what else do you want to know?" she asks after a while.

Before I can censor myself, I say, "What's it like?"

"Oh boy," Hannah says. "The first time is never good, I don't care what your friends tell you. It hurts. Like someone's jabbing a hot knife around your insides. But it gets better after that."

I swallow hard. Hot knife? I'd always heard that there's a little bit of blood, but nobody ever mentioned anything about pain, not even Tabitha.

"But here's the thing," Hannah continues. "The physical stuff—that's not the hard part. It's your emotions that make it messy. When you're that intimate with another person, you become more vulnerable than you ever thought possible. So if you share yourself with someone who isn't worthy of what you're giving . . . it can screw you up, big time."

I want to ask her if she feels like Jack was worthy, considering the current circumstances. But I don't know, asking my brother's girlfriend about their sex life seems wrong, like it's too private a subject to broach. My silence doesn't seem to faze Hannah, who's on a roll.

"It may not always seem like such a big thing when you're doing it. I know I wasn't really thinking about diseases or what happens if the condom breaks. Those were things that happened to other people, you know? It couldn't possibly happen to me.

"Look," she continues. "I'm not trying to scare you into abstinence. I just think you should be informed."

"I know I'm not ready to have . . . sex," I say. "See? I still have trouble saying the *word*."

She laughs. "Definitely a sign."

"I guess maybe I need help learning how *not* to have sex, if that makes sense."

"Ah," Hannah says. "You need boundaries."

"Yes," I say. "Boundaries."

"Talk to Tobin. Be honest with him. Tell him what you told me. Tell him you're not ready."

"But it hasn't even come up yet!"

"Doesn't matter," she says. "He should understand. Sure, he might be uncomfortable, at least at first. But if Tobin is even half the boy you think he is, then he'll not only respect your decision, he'll respect *you* for being so honest about it."

"Honest," I repeat.

"Yes," she says, only it comes out like "Yaarrrssse," because she's yawning at the same time. "I have *got* to go to sleep."

"Yeah," I say. "Me too."

We say good night and restore darkness to the room. I replay bits of our conversation in my head, and as I do, I realize how lucky I am. Hannah was right—honesty is important. Between her and Mom, I couldn't have asked for better counsel.

"Hey, Hannah?"

"Mmm?"

"Thanks," I say. "Not just for the clothes or the conversation, but for everything. I know I wasn't exactly . . . friendly . . . when you first got here. But I'm so glad you *are* here. And I just know you're going to make a great mom."

"Thanks," she says, her voice cracking over the word. "You're pretty cool yourself."

# Chapter 26

Allison finally breaks her silence at lunch.

"What'd you do, raid Tabitha's closet?" she asks snappishly as I lay my tray on the table. "I mean, could that skirt *be* any shorter? I think that hair dye seeped into your brain."

I look down at the all-black outfit I pulled together from the stuff Hannah bought me yesterday, but before I can defend myself, she continues, "God, Lucy, you're so full of yourself."

Now, I'm not quite clear on how a secondhand turtleneck and ribbed miniskirt make me full of myself, but I let it go and slip into my usual seat. Allison rolls her eyes, but at least she doesn't get up and walk away.

I take a tentative bite of the meat product the lunch lady calls burger. It's cold and slimy and tastes like something you'd feed to a household pet. Allison's burger, I notice, has been extracted from its pink, ketchup-stained bun. It just lies there, untouched among a sea of soggy fries. Simply *looking* at this food is making me feel sick.

"I tried to call you last night," I say as I peel the foil

from the top of my apple-juice cup. She drags one of the fries through a runny pool of ranch dressing and doesn't respond. I repeat, "I tried to call you last night."

"I heard you the first time," she says.

"So then why didn't you answer me?"

"Um, because I'm *mad* at you?"

"I know that. But why?"

"Oh, please." Allison snorts. "Like you even have to ask. Why don't you go have lunch with your stupid *boy*friend?"

"What are you talking about?" I say, my voice so loud kids three tables away turn for a look. "Why are you being so mean?"

Her eyes pop. "Me?" she asks. Then her mouth screws up some, and her voice takes on the high-pitched tone Brody uses when he's mocking me: "Tobin's car only seats four people, so why don't you sit at home like the boyfriend-less loser you are!"

As if I didn't already feel bad enough.

"I'm supposed to be your best friend," she continues, her face growing super red, super quick. "And we always said we'd never be the kind of girls who ditched their friends for some guy."

Her blatant hypocrisy causes me to look up from my burger, which I've been stabbing repeatedly with a plastic fork. "You did it," I say. "Is ditching your friends only okay when the guy in question is a lame-ass like Brad Thomas?"

"That's different! You didn't even want to go to homecoming!"

"Of course I wanted to go!" I holler, not even caring about the growing number of fellow diners listening in on our heated exchange.

"That's not what you said. You said—"

In a completely uncharacteristic move, I slam my cup on the table, sending sprays of juice flying. "I don't care what I said—I wanted to go. And you *know* that if a cute older boy asked you to go to the planetarium with him on a Saturday night, you wouldn't run right out and extend the invitation to me." Before she can respond, I get up, turn on my heel, and storm out, neglecting to even dump my tray.

Thankfully, the tears don't come until I've fully exited the cafeteria. I round the corner and head straight for a shadowy patch of hallway at the opening of the north wing, lean the back of my head against the wall, and start to bawl.

The bell rings; I quickly wipe the wet from my cheeks and am trying to think of a nearby hiding place when Tobin materializes a few feet away. He sees me in almost the same second and comes jogging over to me. The smile on his face melts as he gets closer. "Biscuit," he says, and with that one word I break, and the tears return. "What's wrong?"

I can't answer him. I can't even talk, I'm sobbing so hard. Tobin's head bobs up and I catch him scanning the crowd. I'm making *such* the scene. Then he says, "C'mon, let's get out of here."

"Wha-wha-what about class?" I splurt.

He grins. "There'll be another one tomorrow."

I'm about to give in and let him kidnap me for the afternoon when I feel a light tap on my shoulder. Allison. I wipe some wayward tears from my cheeks and breathe deeply.

"Here," she says, handing me my new purse. "I think you forgot this."

"Oh," I say. "Thanks."

"Can we talk for a minute?" Allison asks.

I look up at Tobin, who's nodding, then back at Ally. "Sure."

Tobin squeezes my arm, asks me to meet him at his car after school, and vanishes into a thick crush of students rushing to their next class. The warning bell rings.

"We can't stay here," Allison says.

I follow her out a back door, across the courtyard, and into a relatively roomy supply closet tucked next to the band room. When she pulls the cord on the overhead lightbulb, I realize that we're in the gear shop, this legendary hook-up spot among the band geeks—founded, incidentally, by my very own brother some six years ago. It smells of must and mildew—most likely due to the limp, outdated marching uniforms thrown over a length of rotting twine. Shelves line each wall, overstuffed with old instruments that have been plucked, beaten, and blown into retirement.

A sneeze escapes me. As I wipe my nose with a spare epaulet, Allison mumbles something I think is supposed to pass as an apology.

"What?" I say. "I couldn't hear you."

"I'm sorry I made you cry," she says, her own eyes filling up with tears. "But I hate this. You're my best friend. We've always done everything together. And now I feel like you do everything with Tabitha instead."

"That's not true."

"It feels true." She sniffles; I hand her an epaulet and look away as she cleans up her reddened cheeks. "It's just so hard. I mean, yes, I got to go to homecoming. But you're someone's *girlfriend* now. And not just any someone's—you're Tobin Scacheri's girlfriend. And I'm just this loser who has to stay home every Saturday night while all the girls I *used* to be friends with go out to the movies or the Charcoal Pit or the freaking *planetarium*!" She says this so fast that she's practically out of breath by the time she finishes. More than that, the tears have returned, these fat droplets that race down her face until her skin is completely wet.

"Plus," she continues, "you didn't even tell me about Jack and Hannah and the baby, and I'm supposed to be your best friend!"

"I tried to call you," I say. "Tabitha only found out because I went to her house when you wouldn't come to the phone."

"You told Tabitha first?"

"Well, yeah," I say slowly, feeling a queasiness building in my stomach. "I mean, didn't she tell you?"

Allison shakes her head. "Kim Talbot's cousin Jenna works at the Food-n-Stuff. She overheard Hannah discussing the benefits package with their manager. Between Jenna and Kim just about everyone knows now."

Does "everyone" include Tobin? Even though I haven't gotten around to telling him yet, I figured the news would definitely come from me.

Ally regains her composure for a second time. "Look, I'm *sorry*, Lucy. Honest. I just feel like I'm so far behind you guys. And now this—" She waves her hand, gesturing to my outfit, prompting me to yank my miniskirt a little closer to my knees. "Look at you!" she says. "You're all hip and stylish and going out with this totally gorgeous junior that *everybody* wants. Pretty soon you're not going to even want to be friends with me. Like the Kims and Tabitha."

"Is *that* what this is all about?"

She bites her bottom lip and casts her eyes downward. I take this as an affirmation.

"Of course we're going to stay friends!" I say. "I mean, yeah, Tabitha and I have been spending a lot of time together. But seriously—even when we were getting ready to go to Tobin's party, I swear I was wishing *you* were there."

"Why?"

"Because you know me best, and because you never push me to be something I'm not. No boy is going to change that, even if he *is* Tobin Scacheri."

I say all this to her, and I'm pretty sure I mean it. Before I know it, Allison's long skinny arms are crushing me in a hug, and all is forgiven, at least for now.

# Chapter 27

Although I spring from the building the second the last bell sounds, Tobin is already leaning against the Vomit by the time I reach the junior/senior parking lot. He looks so cool, pressed up against the bumper like that, the wind blowing the strands of his surfer-blond hair.

"Hey, you," he says.

"Hi."

I lift my lips slightly, expecting a kiss, but Tobin bypasses them completely. He takes my backpack from me and opens the passenger-side door. I climb in, slightly confused and disappointed. Tobin slides in his side and starts the car, and over the growl of the engine he says, "Feeling any better?"

"Yeah."

"Wanna talk about it?"

"Not really."

"Oh."

It could be my imagination, but I think he pops the gear into reverse with a little more force than necessary. We lurch from the parking lot and head to my house in complete silence. He doesn't even flick on the radio, and the quiet makes my skin itch.

When we pull up to my house, Tobin doesn't cut the engine right away. Instead, he puts the car into park and pumps the gas lightly. Then, without even looking at me, he says, "So is it that you don't like to talk about things in general, or that you don't like to talk about things with me?"

I'm not sure how to respond to this, so I don't. This seems to make Tobin angrier.

"I mean, you said that there's all this stuff going on," he huffs. "But you won't tell me what this 'stuff' is. And then today I find you crying in the hallway, and you won't tell me what's wrong. It's like you don't want to talk to me at all. Like all you want to do is *kiss*."

He says this last word with such disgust that I can't help laughing. And not a little laugh, either. It starts as a giggle, kind of soft and low, but the absurdity fuels the giggle until it's an all-out, belly-shaking guffaw. I mean, really. Here I am, filled with anxiety over the inevitability of Tobin Scacheri wanting to jump me, and here he is, wanting to *talk*.

"Will you quit laughing?"

"I'm sorry," I say.

"It's not funny."

"I know." I take a deep breath and begin. "You know that girl who drove me to your party? That's my brother's girlfriend, Hannah. She's . . . well, she's pregnant." I pause, waiting for some sort of reaction, but all Tobin does is nod, as if to say, *Go on*.

So I do, right there in the driveway, with the engine idling loudly over my words. He doesn't say much, except for the occasional "Right" or "Wow," which lets me know he's still listening. I tell him all about Jack and Hannah, and how no one seems to know what's going to happen next. I tell him about the fight I had with Allison, and how we made up but I'm not sure how long that will last. I'm about to tell him about Tabitha and her recent breakup with Elliot but stop myself when I remember that Tobin's friends with Spencer, and that Tab might not want her personal business getting back to him through a third party.

When I finish speaking, there's a small smile playing on Tobin's lips. "Thank you," he says. "I don't know if that's the appropriate response, but it's what I feel."

"Why?"

"Because," he says, "it means you trust me."

He shuts the car off, and we head inside. No one's home—except the Brodster, who we can hear yelling at the basement TV through the air vent in the foyer. In the kitchen, I find a note from Mom, asking me to brown some ground beef for a meat sauce. Tobin offers to chop vegetables for the salad, and so we cook, side by side, not saying a word, but at the same time, silently saying more than we have the entire time we've known each other.

Tobin's loading the salad spinner when Brody surfaces from his basement cave. "Are you the boyfriend?" he says to Tobin, making my face feel as red as the sauce I'm defrosting in the microwave.

"Maybe," Tobin says, lifting one eyebrow. "Are you the little brother?"

"Little?" Brody snorts. "I gave *her* a fat lip." He jerks his thumb in my direction. "Didn't I, Lucy?"

"Yeah," I say. "And didn't Mom just ban you from playing Sega for a month?"

"What do you play?" Tobin interjects. "On the Sega, I mean."

The little beast shrugs. "Everything."

"What about the new Dead or Alive game?"

"That Karate one, with the hot girls in it?" Brody rolls his eyes. "Everybody knows that's only on Xbox, duh."

"Right, right," Tobin says. "That's what we have at my house, if you want to come over and check it out sometime."

Now Grody Brody is all abuzz. "Seriously?" he says. "You'd let me do that?"

Tobin grins. "I don't see why not."

Amazing. He's got the snotty bugger eating out of the palm of his hand. While the boys discuss shortcuts and cheat codes, I continue working on the meat sauce and put a pot of water on for the noodles.

Mom comes home, chipper for a change. She sends Brody up to clean his room and asks me and Tobin to set the dining room table so that she can take a quick bath before dinner. Tobin carries the plates and I get the silverware. "Here, let me help," he says, grabbing a handful of knives, forks, and spoons. I notice that he puts the spoon on the left side of the plate, next to the fork, and lays the knives down so that the blade is pointed away from the plate, instead of toward it. When Brody does this, I get totally annoyed, but right now, standing here with Tobin, I find the settings completely charming.

Hannah comes home a few minutes later, looking tired but perking up when she sees Tobin. I formally introduce her to him and she says, "Pleased to make your acquaintance. I've heard many good things about you."

"Yeah?" Tobin says. "I've heard lots of good stuff about you, too."

"If you'll excuse me," Hannah says, "I'm dying to get out of this hideous uniform."

She heads upstairs; Tobin and I are quietly folding

napkins and slipping them under the fork/spoon duos when I hear a key in the lock. It alarms me for a second, because as far as I know, everyone's present and accounted for. But then it hits me.

Jack's come home.

# Chapter 28

I bolt for the front door, and sure enough, there's my older brother, loaded down with his battered duffle and a newish-looking trumpet case. I practically tackle him in a hug, but Jack just pulls away. "Whoa," he says, looking me over. "What did you do to your hair?"

"There was an incident," I say, self-consciously touching the black strands.

"Clearly."

I clear my throat and say, "Where's Dad?"

"Toronto. Is Hannah home?"

Before I can answer, Tobin materializes in the foyer. "Hey, Biscuit," he says. "Where do you keep the trivets?"

If Jack didn't look surprised before, he most certainly does now. *"Biscuit?"* he repeats, eyes locked on me.

Tobin steps forward and waves. "You must be Jack."

Jack turns to face him. "Who are you?"

"This," I say, "is my *boyfriend*, Tobin Scacheri. Tobin, this incredibly rude *child* is my brother."

"Boyfriend?" Jack says. "Since when do you have a boyfriend?"

All three of us are startled to hear Hannah's voice answer. "Since you left," she says, coolly, from the top of the stairs. "What's that?" She extends a slender finger in Jack's direction.

Suddenly, all the attitude my brother had vaporizes. "It's a trumpet," he says.

"I know that," Hannah says. "But it's not the same one you left with, is it?"

Where is my beautiful, peacekeeping mother when we need her? Or even Brody, for god's sake. I shift from one foot to another, not sure who will explode first.

"Well?" Hannah shrills. Her hand is gripping the banister so hard that even I can see that all blood has drained from her knuckles. Jack starts to mumble something when Hannah cuts in, "I can't hear you. You'll have to speak up."

The sharpness of her tone restores some of Jack's bravado. He lifts his chin and says, "It's mine. I bought it in Toronto."

My head swivels back, Ping-Pong style, to catch Hannah's reaction. Her grip doesn't loosen, but her voice becomes even more of a growl.

"I see."

Back to Jack. "The dollar's stronger up there, babe. It was a steal, really. I know we're supposed to be saving, not spending, but I figured it was more like an investment. In our future."

"*Your* future, you mean," Hannah says. She removes her hand from the banister and places it on her stomach. "This," she says tightly, "is *my* future. *Babe*."

My brother tosses me a helpless look—figuring, I suppose, that out of everyone I'm the most likely to give him a little support. Only I can't, because she's right, and he's never been more wrong. Hannah turns in defeat, but not before I see the first of her tears start to fall. I rush to Jack and shove him hard. "How could you?" I shout, not realizing how loud the words are until they echo in my ears. Jack says nothing. He doesn't even push me back. Instead, he lets out a soft sigh, gathers up his bags, and heads for the basement.

My first instinct is to go after Hannah, but then I remember that Tobin's there, and that he's seen and heard it all. In almost the same second I feel his big paw of a hand on my shoulder. He doesn't say anything, just kneads the muscle slightly.

"Tobin?"

"Yeah?"

"Could you maybe take me someplace that isn't here?"

"Let's go."

I walk out without another word, not even pausing to tell my mother where I'm going.

# Chapter 29

Tobin takes me back to his house. I stop crying on the way over, but I'm still all red and splotchy when we go inside. His mother is in the kitchen, elbow deep in potting soil, wrestling with the tangled roots of an enormous jade plant. She looks up from her work, one eyebrow slightly raised. "Early dinner?"

"Actually," Tobin says, "we didn't get to eat."

"Oh?"

"There's some stuff going on at Lucy's house," he tells her. "Is it okay if she hangs here for a while?"

"Of course," Claudia says. "Why don't you grab some of that leftover Stroganoff in the fridge?"

While Tobin fixes us two plates, I excuse myself and retreat to the lime green bathroom to splash some water on my face. When I check the results in the oval mirror hanging over the sink, I am suddenly struck by how much I look like my brother. Both of my brothers, really. We have the same high forehead, the same wide-set blue eyes, the same double dip between the bottoms of our mouths and the curves of our chins. And there's going to be a baby, whether Jack likes it or not, and it's quite possible that baby will look like a miniature us.

*The baby.* Didn't he think of the baby? Babies can't eat trumpets. They can't wear them, either. I think of Hannah, schlepping off to the Food-n-Stuff in her grass green smock, ringing up packs of Parliaments and long strips of lotto tickets, standing on swollen feet for seven or eight hours at a stretch, all because of the baby. And then my brother, traipsing around the continent, too busy playing jazz to even call and check in on Hannah with any frequency.

There's a soft knock at the door. "Luce?" Tobin says. "You okay?"

"Coming."

I shut off the water—and my brain—and leave the shelter of the lime green bathroom. Tobin leads me down the stairs to the basement. We set up camp on a plush couch the color of coffee ice cream. I brace myself, waiting for Tobin to ask me if I want to talk about it, but thankfully he seems to understand that I most certainly do *not*. Instead, he flicks on the TV, and we nibble on the tangy Stronganoff as we watch a doubleheader of *Simpsons* reruns.

And I'm not sure why, but seeing Maggie staple-gun Homer to the wall makes me blurt out, "Are you a virgin?" And it's like one of those movie moments where the girl's trying to tell her friend something private at a party, but she has to shout over the music, and of course that's the split second that the record needle screeches into silence, and whatever embarrassing tidbit she was sharing echoes in everybody's ears. The word just hangs there: "virgin." *"Virgin."* "VIRGIN."

"No," he says finally, without even breaking his gaze from the TV. "Is that a problem?"

"Not really. I mean, I kind of figured."

"Yeah?"

"Yeah."

A string of commercials comes on. Tobin's shoulders are completely rigid. I'm not feeling so very relaxed myself. Then he says, "What about you? Are you a . . . ?"

He can't even say it.

"Of course," I say. "You were the first boy I've even *kissed*, remember?"

"Oh, right," he says, in a voice I can't read.

There are a million directions this conversation could go in—I could ask him who she was, if there was more than one, if he loved her/them, if it bothers him that I haven't—but I don't want to talk anymore. I don't want to think anymore. So I lay my head on his shoulder and feel his tense muscle loosen under it. We snuggle into each other, his arm winding its way across my waist. It's soft and it's warm and it feels so good that I can't concentrate on the television, only the way our bodies fit together.

I lift my face to meet his and we kiss. His mouth still tastes like salty-sweet sauce from the Stroganoff. We twist around a bit, and Tobin's hand grazes my knee a few times before he lets it rest there. Heat shoots out from my knee, spreading up my leg and into the pit of my belly.

But then his hand stirs, moving slowly but steadily, and then it's just there, on my *thigh*, and it's not stopping, but inching higher up, and I don't want it to stop but it has to stop, we have to stop.

I shove his hand off and jerk backward. "I'm not going to sleep with you!" I say, yanking my skirt down as far as it can be yanked. Tobin doesn't say a word, just sits there, wide-eyed and panting hard, like he's just done the hundred-yard dash. "I'm not," I repeat, a bit more calmly. "I won't."

"Ever?"

"Well, not *ever*. But definitely not *now*." I catch my top lip between my teeth and bite hard. Tobin stays mute. Finally, I say, "Are you going to break up with me?"

Tobin chuckles. "Yes, Lucy. That's exactly what I'm going to do. It's what I do to every girl who won't spread her legs within the first month of us even knowing each other."

Sarcasm. I think.

"Of course I'm not breaking up with you," he continues. "Give me some credit. If all I wanted was action, I wouldn't date you." I must make a face because then he says softly, "You know what I mean."

"Yeah," I say. "I guess."

Tobin scratches his fingers through his hair and shakes his head. "Hey," he says, giving me one of those sly half smiles. "We okay?"

Okay? When he looks at me like that, I feel like there's a big fat hamster running a marathon in my chest.

"Yeah," I say. "We're good."

He kisses the tip of my nose. "Would it make you feel better if we set some ground rules? You know, so we're both clear on what's fair game?"

*Boundaries.*

"If you want," I say, coolly, like there's *not* a hamster motoring my heart.

Tobin grins. "Let's start with kissing—kissing's allowed, right?"

"Yes," I say. "Definitely."

"What about touching?"

I shiver involuntarily. "Depends."

"On what?"

"Location."

He lifts a finger and gently slides it down my cheek. "What about here?" he asks. "Is here good?"

"Mmm-hmm."

The finger slides to my bottom lip. "Here?" I nod. Slowly, Tobin drops his hand to my hyperactive heart and lays his palm flat on it. "This okay?" he murmurs.

I let out a soft sigh. "Sure," I say. "I mean, I guess so." His hand migrates a little to the left and down an inch or so. My breath freezes in my rib cage.

"Is it okay if I touch you here?" Tobin whispers, breath hot against my ear. He's trembling slightly, or maybe it's me.

"Sometimes," I whisper back. "Sometimes you can touch me there."

Tobin draws a deep breath and I feel his hand slip down to my stomach, grazing the surface of my shirt but not stopping. "How about—"

"No," I say, gently pushing his hand back to his own lap. "Not there. Not yet."

"Okay," he says. "Good to know."

The hamster hasn't slowed much, and the pink flush in Tobin's cheeks makes me wonder if he's feeling the same way.

"Lucy!" Tobin's mom calls out, her voice like a vat of ice water over our heads. "There's someone here to see you!"

Tobin shoots me a quizzical look, and I shrug.

"Even if they thought I was at your house, no one knows where you live," I say.

"Except Hannah," he reminds me.

Right.

I pull myself off the couch, square my shoulders, and troop up the stairs like a good soldier heading into battle. The landing is clear, so I creep out into the foyer. That's when I see that it's not Hannah who's come to fetch me, but Jack, standing alone in the rain, wet hair dripping into his eyes.

"Can we talk?"

# Chapter 30

Jack drives slowly through the slick streets of the neighborhoods in our town. We drive into Old New Castle, up to the wharf, and around again. We drive past Haley High, past the offices of the *Daily Journal*, through the corporate park to Route 273, and over near the Food-n-Stuff where Hannah now works. It's here that Jack finally speaks: "I don't think she'll go back to California. Just so you know. Her mom's kind of a flake. She means well, but she and Hannah are more like friends than mother and daughter. Hannah needs more support than that."

"She needs you," I say quietly. "And you screwed up, big-time."

"I know that."

"But *why?*"

Jack sighs, and eases the van into the empty parking lot of a bank. "That, I don't know."

"That's not good enough."

"I don't know what else to tell you."

We sit there, not talking, watching the rain coat the windshield. I close my eyes, wishing I had the magic to make it all go away.

"It wasn't supposed to be like this." Jack's voice yanks me back, and I look at him, but he's turned away, staring out the window. "We had decided to get . . . we'd decided not to have it. That's why I sold my trumpet. But then when we went to that place—the clinic—she couldn't go through with it.

"So we came home. We were going to live here, get jobs, do the responsible parent thing. But then Dad asked me to go with them on the road, and I was out there, playing the trumpet and living the life, and I loved it. I've always loved it. Music's in my blood. *You* know that. I know you know that."

"Yeah," I say. "I do."

"I'm not ready to give that up." Slowly he turns back to me, keeping his eyes down, avoiding mine.

"But I don't get it, Jack. Why would you have to? I mean, why does it have to be all or nothing? Couldn't you just put the music thing on hold for a while?"

"No," he says slowly. "I couldn't."

"Yes, you could."

"You don't get it," he says. "I don't *want* to."

"Oh."

And that's when he starts to cry. Not just a little, either. Enormous boy tears skate down his cheeks in rapid succession. I look at him, all broken and blubbery. My big brother. I don't know that I've ever seen him cry.

"I'm sorry," he croaks, his voice sounding sore from the tears.

I get the feeling that I'm not the one he's really apologizing to, but I still say it's okay, even though it isn't, and I say I understand, even though I don't.

"Thanks," he says, but it's a hollow thanks and sounds almost as fake as the things I've just said.

It takes a while for Jack to regain his composure, but eventually he does. He smears his nose on his sleeve, kicks the wipers into high gear, and drives the two of us home.

By the time we get there, it's about midnight. Jack slumps off to the basement, and I quietly creep up the stairs. A bit of light seeps out through the crack under my parents' bedroom door, and for one brief moment, I feel the need to knock, to ask Mom if I can sleep with her tonight. But I'm too old for that, and I know it, and what's worse, I feel it now more than ever.

The door to my own dark room is open, and for a second I think it might be empty. I walk in slowly, steeling myself for Hannah's absence, but she's in there, on her bed, lying on her back.

"Hey," she says.

"Hi."

"So you *were* at Tobin's?"

"Yeah," I say. "Jack came and got me."

"I know. I told him where to find you."

"That's why," I say.

"Why what?"

"Why you can't go."

She sits up. "How do you figure?"

"Because," I say, "you're the one who knows where to find me." My voice cracks on "me," and I begin to weep, and then she starts in, and she stretches her arms out and I fall into them, and we cry all over each other. And the weird part is, I now feel closer to her than I do to my own brother.

"If anyone should leave, it should be him," I say.

"No," Hannah says. "Don't say that."

"But it's true."

"No. He's your brother."

"So? You're my family, too."

This only makes her cry harder, and that makes *me* cry harder, and all the crying hurts my eyes and my lungs, but at the same time it feels really good, like when you're finally able to throw up whatever's making you feel so sick.

Hannah strokes my hair. "You remember when you told me I'd make a good mom? Well, the way Jack talks about you . . . He's going to be a good dad someday. He just—"

"What?"

"He needs time to be a good man."

# Chapter 31

I can't sleep. My alarm clock tells me it's almost four A.M., and I haven't slept a single second. Through the darkness, I peer over at Hannah, but if she's tossing and turning, I certainly can't tell. With a frustrated sigh, I throw my covers off, slip out of the bed, and head down the stairs to the kitchen.

Where I find Jack.

"Can't sleep?" He absentmindedly dunks a cookie into a mug of what looks like milk.

"No," I say. "You?"

"Nope."

We stare at each other across the space between us—a space that feels wider by the second.

Jack shoves the rest of the cookie into his mouth. "Go put your shoes on."

"Where are we going?"

"You'll see."

Jack eases the van into a parking spot that's dead center of the wharf. A couple of other vehicles are parked there, with windows so steamy you can't see inside. We get out; Jack starts walking like he knows exactly where he's going, so I follow him and try to keep up with his large strides.

The air is cold and we can see our breath as we trek along the path that winds through Battery Park. I have a feeling we shouldn't be out so late—or rather, so *early*—but the sting of the air feels good in my lungs. Cleansing, even. I look over at Jack. His hands are jammed deep inside his pockets and he's staring at the ground directly in front of his feet.

"Um, Jack?"

"Yeah?"

"Where are we going?"

"Just keep walking."

We cross the entire length of the park. Jack turns on his heel and I think we're about to retrace our path when he hoists himself onto a nearby bench. I stand a few feet in front of him, shifting my weight from side to side, my shoes squishing into grass still wet from the rainstorm earlier tonight.

"I miss this place," he says finally. "Nearly every meaningful thing that ever happened to me happened here in this park."

*Except meeting Hannah*, I think, but don't dare say it out loud.

Jack sighs. "I know what you think I should do

about the . . . situation. Baby. Whatever. I know what everyone thinks I should do, who I should be. I thought I could be that person, but . . ."

"But?"

"But I'm not."

I peer at Jack through the dim light that washes over the park from the power plant across the river. He's picking at the plastic bit that covers the end of one of his shoelaces; his hair, badly in need of a trim, falls into his eyes. He looks small and sort of nervous. Not at all like the big strong brother I've missed all these months.

"I keep picturing her face when I told her about the trumpet. I've never seen her so angry."

"Can you blame her?"

Jack looks up, startled. "Nah, not really." He takes a deep breath, lets it out slowly. "Tonight, when I couldn't sleep, I started thinking about what you said. How it doesn't have to be all or nothing. It would be easier if it did, but it doesn't."

"What do you mean?"

"That I've been a selfish ass."

The sharpness of his words takes me by surprise. I wait for him to say more; when he doesn't, I say, "You brought me to the park at four in the morning to tell me you've been a selfish a—"

"Hey," he says, cutting me off. "Watch your language."

"Yes, *Dad*," I say, which is what I always say when he lectures me, but tonight I don't even realize what I've said until the words are already out, hanging over my head like one of those bubbles in a paneled comic strip. "Oh, Jack. I didn't mean—"

"Don't sweat it." Jack blows on his naked hands and rubs them together for warmth. "So do you remember when I was applying to schools, and I'd heard from every place except Berklee?"

"Not really," I admit.

"Well," he says, "I'd just decided to go to U Penn when I got the call from Berklee. Dad was psyched, but Mom kept saying I should go to U Penn, because I could get certified to teach there. Like some sort of fallback plan, if I couldn't hack it on the road.

"When I was in Canada I started thinking about Penn. I mean, completely different program, heavy emphasis on theory, not quite as progressive. But it's a solid school. And it's only about forty minutes away from here."

It takes a few minutes for what he says to begin to sink in.

"I figure I can finish out the year in Boston. I'd get out of classes just in time for . . . for the birth. And then, I don't know, I could take a semester off or something. But eventually I could transfer to Penn. It's not ideal, but I'd certainly feel like less of an asshole."

I guess I'm supposed to be turning cartwheels, but I'm not. Instead, I say quietly, "She deserves better. You know that, don't you?"

"Christ, Lucy!" Jack cries. "What do you want from me? I'm twenty years old and all I'm qualified to do is blow my horn."

"Daddy was only two years older when he and Mom had you."

"Well, I'm not 'Daddy,' " he says bitterly. "I'm me. And this is the best I can do. For now, at least." He hops down off the bench. "I don't know why I thought you'd understand. You're just a kid."

"I understand plenty."

"Sure," he says. "You're fourteen, you know everything."

He looks so angry, not just at me but at the whole world. I stand there, trying to see things through his eyes, but I can't. All I see is Hannah, curled up and crying on the bed. I wonder if she used to believe in my brother as much as I did.

"We should head home," Jack says. "You've got school tomorrow, right?" I don't respond, just follow a few steps behind as we trek back to the van.

We drive back to the house in silence. No talk, no radio, nothing. When we pull into the driveway, Jack reaches over and puts his hand on my arm. "I never said I was perfect."

"I know."

But I didn't know, not until tonight. I think of what Hannah said, about Jack needing time to become a good man, and how it must be hard enough for my brother, who's really just a boy, to simply be a man.

# Chapter 32

Tension runs rampant through our house over the next few days, especially after Dad comes home. There are many, many discussions, between my parents, between Jack and Hannah, and various other combinations of the four of them, nearly all of which are held behind closed doors. The only bit of information I've gleaned is that Jack and Hannah have decided they aren't going to be boyfriend-girlfriend for a while. Except there have been two times since the supposed breakup that Hannah has snuck out of my room and not returned until morning. So, who knows?

Then, on Saturday, Mom asks me if I'd like to go with her to get some coffee and talk.

"Since when do you drink coffee?" I ask her.

"Since the chamomile stopped working," she replies. "I figure if I can't find a way to calm my nerves, I might as well make sure they're at optimum energy."

"Oh."

We drive all the way up to Concord Pike. Mom's kind of distracted as she drives; she rambles on about

Thanksgiving, which is only two weeks away, and do I want to invite Tobin and his mother over for dessert?

"Really?" I say, grinning. "That would be great!"

We pull into the parking lot of the shopping center and head into Brew-Ha-Ha. Mom orders a pumpkin spice with soy; I opt for a double caramel latte. We get our drinks and head over to a small table in the corner of the café.

"So what's up, Mom?" I say. "Why the big coffee conference?"

She blows across the top of her mug and says, "I was wondering how you felt about the basement."

"What about the basement?"

"How would you like to move into it?"

"Why would I want to do that?"

"Because," Mom says, "then you could have your own room again."

I'm confused at first, because Mom's being so vague. But then it hits me.

"Oh my god!" I squeal. "Is she really staying?"

"Yes." Mom smiles. "For a while, anyway. Definitely until after the baby's born. Which is why you get the basement—it gets a little damp when it rains, and I'd feel more comfortable knowing Hannah's completely warm and dry."

"What about Jack?"

"Hannah approved his Boston-until-birth plan. He

can bunk with Brody when he comes home next May."

I slurp down some of my latte, trying to absorb all this reshuffling.

"We're going to have a lot of work to do," Mom says. "I figured you might want to paint the basement, get a new rug—you know, give it a little makeover."

"Really?"

Mom nods. "And then there's the nursery."

I'm not sure what she's talking about at first, because I think all rooms in the house are now accounted for. Except—

"Oh, Mom," I say. "Your darkroom."

"It's okay. I'll make do."

I remember when Mom had the darkroom built. It was right after she was promoted to managing photo editor, which meant a bigger salary. It took her months to finalize the plans and get the setup exactly the way she wanted it. Once it was completed, I'd often catch her standing at the doorway, peeking inside and grinning, so happy to finally have a space that was all her own.

"It's not fair," I say after a pause.

"Explain, please."

"I don't get why you have to give up your darkroom, and Hannah has to give up school, and Jack gets off so easy."

Mom sighs gently. "No one's getting off easy, Lucy. I know it may seem like Jack's not making any great sacrifice, but to be fair, Berklee's been his dream since he was younger than Brody. Don't get me wrong—I'm not thrilled about some of the decisions he's made— but I think he's trying, in his own way."

*He should be trying harder,* I think.

"Besides," she says, "your dad's looking into better job openings for Hannah down at the university. He thinks he can get her benefits and free tuition, so the Food-n-Stuff gig shouldn't last too much longer and a degree certainly isn't out of the question."

"Well, that's good," I say. "But it still feels . . . uneven."

Mom nods, and we finish our coffees in silence.

# Chapter 33

I'm sleeping soundly when my mother barges in my door and wakes me from this bizarre dream. Tobin and I were on a tropical island, dancing to this wild calypso music. Jack was on a stage, blowing his trumpet, moving around to the rhythm of the steel drum. Brody was standing near Jack, smacking a tambourine out of sync.

I couldn't see Hannah, but I have a feeling she was there, too.

Anyway, Tobin was just about to dream-kiss me when Mom starts hollering, "Lucy Alexis, you better get your lazy butt out of bed and into my kitchen! There are five pounds of potatoes waiting to be peeled!"

She slams on the lights and storms back downstairs. How amazingly rude. Holidays never fail to bring out the worst in my mother. Give her a high-profile perp walk to shoot at five in the morning down at the courthouse and she's unflappable. But throw a turkey into the equation and she's nuttier than a cheese log. Then again, maybe I'd prefer photographing serial killers to fending off Grammy Doyle's incessant nagging, too.

I've never been a huge fan of Thanksgiving, and this one's going to be tougher than most. Dad's driving Jack back to Boston tomorrow. A guy Jack knows from Berklee called last week and asked him if he wanted in on a semiregular gig at Ryles, this big jazz club in Cambridge. He wasn't going to go back until after Christmas, just before the start of spring semester, but apparently playing at this place is some kind of rite of passage. So he's leaving early. He says it will be good, give him extra time to find a job that will work around the insane schedule Berklee expects its students to keep, but secretly I think this is more proof of his selfishness.

Things are still kind of awkward between Jack and me, but I guess that's to be expected. Still, it's been nice having him around these past few weeks. He's been less moody, more relaxed. And last Sunday, when we had Tobin over for dinner, Jack went out of his way to be really nice to him, asking about his car and school and stuff.

Mom's all the way downstairs, but I can still hear her shouting. So I yawn and I stretch, and I pull myself out from under the covers and lumber down to the kitchen. There's a bowl of oatmeal waiting for me on the table; Brody's already halfway through his. A couple of months ago, I wouldn't have eaten anything that Grody Brody had unsupervised access to, but he's . . . different these days. All because of Tobin, who has the kid wrapped around his finger. My entire life, I've tried to get him to quit eating his boogers, and all Tobin had to say is, "Dude, that's gross," and I haven't seen him do it since.

"It's about time," Mom growls as she stuffs herbed butter underneath the skin of our twenty-five-pound bird. "Those potatoes aren't going to peel themselves."

"Oh, pipe down," I say, kissing her on the cheek.

"Is that any way to talk to your mother?" she retorts, but I see her grin nonetheless.

The oatmeal is cold and congealed, and I give up after two lumpy mouthfuls. "Where is everyone, anyway?"

"Dad's getting Grammy," she grunts, still forcing the butter. "And Jack took Hannah on a wild hunt for pecans."

I shake my head. "Do you think this breakup will last?"

"I hope not," Brody pipes up. "I kind of like having her around."

"Really?" I say.

"Don't you?"

"Yeah. Yeah, I do."

I start to attack the potatoes; I've gotten through about three when the phone rings. "I'll get it!" I holler, dodging Mom and grabbing the phone off its cradle.

"Doyle residence."

"Hey, beautiful," Tobin says. Over these past three weeks, beautiful has beaten out Biscuit for his nickname of choice. Not that I'm complaining. "Happy Turkey Day. Did you watch the parade?"

"Nah," I say. "I just got up, actually. I had this . . . uh . . . dream. About you."

"Oh, really?" Tobin says, and I can actually hear him grinning for thirty seconds before Mom snatches the phone out of my hand.

"Tobin, darling, Lucy will have to talk to you later as she is severely behind in her potato-peeling duties and— Yes, that's right, after dinner. Try to get here around six, that's when we'll be having dessert."

"C'mon, Mom!" I am trying to reclaim the phone but she's super quick. "Can't I at least say goodbye?"

Mom holds the phone up and I shout into it, "Bye, Tobin! See you tonight!"

I've barely finished two more potatoes when the phone rings again. "Sweet Jesus!" Mom shouts. "Lucy, I swear to god I'm going to smash that thing to bits."

"I told you I need my own line."

She ignores me and instructs Brody to get the phone and take a message. It's Tabitha, confirming that she and Spencer are coming over postdessert. Not two seconds after Brody hangs up, the phone rings yet again (Allison, also confirming her attendance). In the midst of this craziness, Jack and Hannah burst through the back door. "Huzzah!" Jack shouts. "We got the nuts. We had to clean out every supermarket in a fifteen-mile radius, but we got 'em."

"Good," Mom says. She lifts her knife and points it in Jack's direction. "You, chop the nuts." To Hannah she says, "You, off your feet and will you please eat something? Brody! Bring me the mushrooms! Let's move, people! Move!"

Hannah and I exchange looks, then bust out giggling. She whispers in my ear, "Is she always this crazy at Thanksgiving?"

"This is nothing," I say. "Just wait until Christmas. It'll be even worse, too, 'cause of your mom coming out."

"Oh lord."

The next two hours fly by like nothing, even though Mom shouts, "Time check!" every ten minutes or so. At one point, Jack, clad in a "Don't You Dare Kiss This Cook" apron, hollers, "Brody, go long!" and sails a foot-long French baguette cleanly over my head. Only Jack must've surprised him, because Brody actually ducks, and the bread smacks into a picture frame, knocks it off its hook, and sends it flying to the floor. Upon impact the frame's glass shatters, sending shards across the hardwood. All of us stop cold as Mom makes her way over to the mess.

Because our house is a virtual museum of my mother's photography, I can't remember exactly which picture the demolished frame held. I'm peering over at Mom when she murmurs an "Oh dear," and holds up the print: a five-by-seven version of last year's holiday family portrait. There's a huge white slice running across its center.

"I killed it," Jack says. "I'm so sorry."

But Mom just shrugs. "It's okay," she says. "We were about due for a new one anyway."

And that's when it hits me. My family, which for so long has consisted solely of me, my parents, and my two brothers, has officially expanded. There's a new person in our home, and soon there will be another. But it's not just the house that's changed. It's my life. All of our lives. This time last year, there was no Tobin to invite over for dessert. The Kims were still my friends, I was still a bland shade of blond, and Brody was still eating his boogers.

It amazes me that in a single year—no, in a single *month*—things can become so completely upside down. Or maybe they've become right side up. Just a few weeks ago I felt miserable because everyone was changing—except me. But then I started changing too, and now I'm semiblissful *because* of all those changes, not in spite of them. And I can only wonder what changes this next year will bring.

I can't wait to find out.

# About the Author

Lara M. Zeises holds a Master of Fine Arts degree in creative writing from Emerson College, where she began writing *Contents Under Pressure* as her thesis project. She is also the author of *Bringing Up the Bones*, which was a Delacorte Press Prize Honor Book for a First Young Adult Novel. She lives in Delaware, where she grew up, but you can visit her online at www.zeisgeist.com.

# Acknowledgments

I started working on *Contents Under Pressure* my first semester as a master's degree candidate at Emerson College, in an adolescent novel workshop. Noted picture book author Lisa Jahn-Clough taught the class, and it is because of her passion for all of children's literature that I, too, fell in love with the genre. Lisa, I simply cannot thank you enough for your wisdom, generosity, and friendship.

I owe so much to my editor, Jodi Kreitzman, for having such a sharp eye, and for giving me zillions of insightful comments that helped me excavate the story I truly wanted to tell. And of course, I'm grateful to my agent, George Nicholson, for having faith in me and my work, as well as his assistant, Paul Rodeen, for being such a *mensch.*

Many props to Laurie Faria Stolarz and Steven Goldman, both of whom read countless drafts of this manuscript and provided critical feedback during virtually every stage of the process. (I would be so lost without you guys.) Also to Tea Benduhn and Kim Ablon Whitney, as well as the dozens of other

Emersonians who took the time to read and critique various bits and pieces and full-on drafts.

I would also like to offer my sincerest gratitude to the following: Myra McLarey, for her advice and enthusiasm; Sarah Charnik, for constantly asking, "Did you finish it yet?"; my aunt Barbara, for having "the gene"; the Junior Mafia (especially Chris, Bec, and Marla), for their admirable and often subversive efforts in PR; and last (but never least), my Momma, for giving me life, love, and laughter, as well as more eccentricities than I care to count. You're more than my mother—you're also my friend.